WAKE UP WITH A WITH A STRANGER

ALSO BY FLETCHER FLORA

Blow Hot, Blow Cold
Desperate Asylum
Hildegarde Withers Makes the Scene (with Stuart Palmer)
Killing Cousins
Leave Her To Hell
Let Me Kill You, Sweetheart
Lysistrata
Most Likely To Love
Park Avenue Tramp
Skuldoggery
Strange Sisters
Take Me Home
The Brass Bed
The Devil's Cook
The Hot Shot
The Irrepressible Peccadillo
The Seducer
Wake Up With a Stranger
Whispers of the Flesh

WAKE UP WITH A STRANGER

FLETCHER FLORA

*Special Bonus Edition—includes
the short story "Murder of a Mouse"!*

WILDSIDE PRESS

Published by Wildside Press LLC.
www.wildsidebooks.com

CONTENTS

CHAPTER I

We have this young woman, this Donna Buchanan, who awakened one morning in a room in a house in Midland City, a certain kind of person with a certain kind of day ahead of her.

At first, immediately after opening her eyes, she had a feeling that it was very late and that she would have to get up at once and go down to the shop in which she worked. Then, with increasing awareness of which day it was, she remembered that it was Sunday and that it would not be necessary to get up until she chose, or to go anywhere at all. With this established—the day and the limits of its claims upon her—she was prepared to establish also in her mind the significant sequence of events which had determined that she should awaken here and now instead of somewhere else at another time.

To start with, she thought, *there was the sale of the original peau de soie with the bouffant skirt. I designed it myself and made it myself and sold it myself to no one but Mrs. William Walter Tyler, Queen Harriet herself, the snotty bitch, but I'll have to hand it to her that she's got the body to wear it and get away with it, not all points and edges like some of them. It was the sheerest bit of good luck that the gown was available when she stopped in the shop, just finished and hanging on the rack in the back room as if it were made for her and meant for her from the beginning. But even so, even with such a beautiful chance to show it for the first time, I almost didn't do it because I was afraid. I was afraid she wouldn't like it—and if she hadn't, if she'd rejected it, I'd have hated her guts, I swear to God I'd have scratched her eyes out. But I needn't have been afraid at all as it turned out, because she liked it and bought it, and this is much more important than might at first be apparent. Quite apart from the price, which was four hundred dollars and therefore of considerable importance in itself, there is the matter of having the continuing patronage of Mrs. William Walter Tyler, Queen Harriet, beautiful Hattie, and the additional patronage of all the points and edges who try to look like Hattie and act like Hattie in all that Hattie does for public observation. What Hattie does that is not for public observation is no business or concern of mine, but just the same, in passing, I wonder who the hell she thinks she's fooling with her sly caresses under the guise of feeling the material, and I wonder what the hell kind of life Mr. William Walter Tyler has in bed at home.*

Let's see, now. What happened next in the day that was yesterday and had everything to do with the day that is today? After Queen Hattie had gone, it was quite late, almost time to close the shop, and I went into the back room again, and the sewing machine was running, and because of the sale of the peau de soie, which was the best thing I have ever done and actually worth more than the four hundred dollars it brought, the sound of the sewing machine was like a song, a serenade, a singing in the blood. Gussie was waiting for me there, and I could tell from her excitement that she had been spying through the curtains and had followed the sale right from Queen Hattie in mink to her panties and back, and she asked me if I'd really sold it, the peau de soie, and I told her I had, casually, as if it were nothing unusual at all to have one of my little creations covering the velveteen tail of Mrs. William Walter Tyler, and just about then Aaron came back from wherever he'd been, and I told him about it.

He was happy. He was happy for me, and there's that about Aaron. There was profit in it for him, because it's his shop, but he was basically glad because it was my design and my gown and might be for me the beginning of acceptance and recognition and something truly big at last. He was happier for me than for himself, and there's that about him.

"It's marvelous, Donna," he said. "I am so happy for you."

"Maybe it won't mean anything," I said. "Maybe it's a four-hundred-dollar sale and nothing more."

"Oh, no," he said. "It's a beautiful gown, and it will make Mrs. Tyler look beautiful, and everyone will tell her so, and she'll surely be back for more Donna Buchanan originals. Make no mistake about that."

"Well, I hope you're right," I said, and he said, "It's absolutely true, and you'll see, and we should do something to celebrate it."

He was very sweet with his gray curly hair and soft smiling mouth, and I agreed that it was something that should be celebrated, and after Gussie and the seamstress were gone we talked about what would be a proper celebration and finally decided to go to dinner as a beginning, which we did. I didn't want to go to my apartment even long enough to change clothes, so I changed into my dress shoes and borrowed from the racks the crimson sheath that fitted my mood, and changed in one of the dressing rooms, and we went out and had dinner and later went dancing and got a little drunk on too many brandies, and I could tell that he wanted me, and after a while I began to want him also, though not so much as he wanted me, and eventually we came here to his home, his wife having gone to Florida, and we undressed and went to bed, and so here I am, in bed still, but he is not, for some reason or other, and I wonder why everything is so exceptionally quiet.

Having thus reviewed her way to bed, she lay and listened to oppressive silence, and all at once, for no reason that she could isolate, she was uneasy and a little depressed and no longer so pleased by remembrance of the sale of the peau de soie. Lying quite still, hardly breathing so that her breath would not disturb the air, she listened intently for the sound of Aaron in the bathroom, but she heard no sound at all, and she began to wonder where he could possibly have gone to. It was certainly not reasonable that he would simply get up and go away under the circumstances, leaving her asleep and naked in bed with no word whatever. Unless, of course, he had been called away quite early and planned to return quickly, in which case he would surely have left a note explaining things.

Thinking that this was what he had done, she sat up suddenly and snapped on the small lamp on the table beside the bed. But there was no note on the table or pinned to his pillow, and neither, she learned by leaning to the side and peering over the edge of the bed, had it accidentally fallen to the floor. It was certainly peculiar, and she couldn't understand it at all, and she began to feel a little angry, as well as lonely and depressed, and she would give Aaron hell for it when he returned, you could depend on that, and what made his absence even worse and absolutely inexcusable was that she was becoming increasingly conscious of her own body and wanted him to return for more reasons than one.

Then it occurred to her that he had probably gone downstairs to the kitchen to prepare them some breakfast. This was a perfectly rational and acceptable explanation, because it was just the kind of considerate thing he would do, and she lay and listened intently again, trying to detect the sounds of movement on the lower floor, but she still heard nothing and had really expected to hear nothing, for in so large a house the kitchen was much too far away for sounds to carry. Moving abruptly, she swung her legs over the edge of the bed and reached for her glasses on the bedside table and put them on.

She did not do this because she needed them to see well, but because they had become to her the symbol of something she had never quite isolated and identified, and they gave her a feeling of strength and security and of being the kind of person she wanted to be. They were harlequin-shaped horn rims with plain glass lenses. The optometrist had reported she did not need glasses, but she had insisted so vehemently upon having them that he had finally shrugged and put the plain glass in the frames of her choice. She had thought then, and still thought, that the frames accentuated the natural slant of her eyes and the piquancy of her thin face, and what she thought was true. She was pretty enough without them, but with them she was much more than pretty, and it would have been difficult to determine precisely the substance of the difference.

Wearing the glasses and no more, she walked across the room to a bank of windows and pulled the heavy gray drapes a little apart and stood looking down across a side yard at an angle to the street. It was snowing thickly, great wet flakes, and that explained, in part, the oppressive silence. Houses always went silent, it seemed, in a snow, and even if there were talking and laughing and music, the silence was still there on the inside if the snow was outside.

She crossed to the bathroom and went through it and into the bedroom beyond, the room of Aaron's wife. It gave her a feeling of aggressive pride to be there, a kind of arrogant and insolent sense of triumph to walk naked through the room—a woman wanted, and had, and essential, among the possessions of a woman unwanted and no longer worth having and essential to no one on earth. She sat on the bed, lay back and rolled over on it, got up and went over to the dressing table, and examined the articles on it. If the cosmetics were the right shade, she thought, she might use them to repair the composition of her own face, but they were, of course, much too pastel for her vividness, and she replaced them with an abrupt little gesture of contempt, as if there were necessarily something deficient in a woman who used pastel shades.

Leaning forward, she switched on a light beside the long mirror and studied her body in the shining glass, the high breasts and flat belly and hips that were perhaps a trifle narrow but swelling sufficiently, nevertheless into long clean flanks. Pivoting, she twisted her head arid looked around over her shoulder into the mirror at her backside; and she laughed suddenly and softly and spontaneously at the sight, as if she couldn't help it in the warm, possessive pleasure she felt in herself. But in this warm reaction there was also an element of sadness, the knowledge not specifically recognized that even self-love and self-possession were not inviolable securities, and that she would in time as surely lose herself—at least herself as she was in the glass—as she had lost and would lose others. This understanding, though not clearly verbalized or accepted, took much of the pleasure from her narcissm, and she turned off the light and went back into the bathroom.

Above the lavatory was a large mirrored door, and she opened it and regarded the articles on the shelves. Most of them were masculine—Aaron's possessions, a razor, a can of lather, talcum and lotion and styptic. There was also a bottle of aspirin tablets, and this reminded her that she didn't even have a headache, after having drunk really quite a lot last night, and she felt a little proud that this was the case, as if it were some superiority in herself that made it possible.

Beside the aspirin bottle was a smaller clear cylinder, with cotton under the cork and some very tiny tablets under the cotton. Taking it in her hands, she turned it around and read the word **NITROGLYCERIN** on the small label that had been turned toward the back of the cabinet. She replaced the cylinder and closed the mirrored door and decided that she would take a shower.

From a drawer of a built-in cabinet she took a towel, and from another she took a rubber cap to keep her hair dry. In the tub, she kept increasing the hot water until it was very hot indeed, and after it was so hot that she thought she could stand it no hotter, she turned it off entirely, leaving only the cold water running, and it was then, for the seconds she stood under it, an excruciatingly delightful torture, like a thousand thin needles piercing her flesh. Out of the tub, she rubbed herself dry and went back into Aaron's bedroom to get her clothes.

She found them in a pile on the floor at the foot of the bed, and she separated them and examined them now to see if she had done them any real harm, the crimson sheath and the wisps of nylon, and she was relieved to see that she hadn't. The crimson sheath was rather ridiculous now at mid-morning, but it wouldn't matter in the house or under her coat when she left, and she would stop by the shop and change back into her own dress on the way home. A more serious problem were her shoes, hardly more than thin soles with narrow strategic straps. They were not at all suitable for snow, and she had no galoshes, but since Aaron would deliver her to the shop, it would only be a matter of a few steps in approaching and leaving the car.

Fully dressed, she found her purse and removed her lipstick and went back into the bathroom to do her lips before the mirror, leaning forward and carefully extending and perfecting their natural outline with the vivid color. In doing this, she noticed for the first time that she had neglected to put her glasses back on again after the shower. They were still lying on the edge of the lavatory, and she put them on and studied her face for a moment in the glass and then returned to the bedroom. Now, having run out of things to do, she was forced to consider again the absence of Aaron.

She could not understand it, she simply could not, and the more she thought about it, the more furious she became. Well, if he thought she was going to sit and sit and wait and wait until he got goddamn good and ready to return, he was crazy. What she was going to do, thin shoes or no shoes at all, was go down and get her coat where she had left it below in the hall, call a taxi, and go to the shop and home by herself—and Aaron, the bastard, could go to hell.

Determined to follow this course of action, she went into the hall and began to descend the stairs, and she was halfway down when she understood at last why it was that he had left, and where he had gone, and why he would not return, not today or tomorrow or ever.

He was lying on the floor of the hall below her. He was obviously and incredibly and terrifyingly dead.

2

Aaron Burns was born in a town downstate forty-eight years before he died in his home in St. Louis. His father was an old-fashioned orthodox Jew who operated a haberdashery and prospered at it. He was a stern man, adhering strictly to the tenets of his religion and the mores of his people, but he was also compassionate and just, with compassion tempering justice more often than otherwise. Aaron respected his father, and even loved him in a way, but he often could not understand him and later could not follow him.

The Jewish population of the town was quite small, but it supported one synagogue. Aaron went there to worship, and when he was old enough he started attending public school. It was then that his personality began to develop in a certain way and to acquire a particular quality, and the quality that it began to acquire was bitterness. This was not overt and offensive, as it might have been in a boy less naturally gentle; and instead of becoming the basis of aggression it showed in his eyes and attitude more as a kind of inexplicable sadness than anything else. This quality was not the result of persecution, for there was none, but of exclusion. To be sure, he had fully the acceptance of his own people, and even up to a point the acceptance of the non-Jews, but this was for him too narrow on the one hand and too qualified on the other, and on neither hand was it enough.

He was a bright boy and did well in school, and when he was seventeen he went away to the state university. His academic status there Was exceptionally good, but his social status was essentially the same as it had been at home, and while this was comfortable, it was not sufficient. He finished two years and began a third, and then one morning, without any warning, he quietly packed his things and went home. His father did not question the decision nor ever ask afterward why it had been made. He did not feel compelled or qualified to do the one, and it was unnecessary to do the other. He was certain that he knew without asking.

Aaron went to work in the haberdashery and did as well in the business as he had done in school. He worked there for five years, and in the third year his mother died, and at the end of the fifth his father died also. His father's assets were far greater than Aaron had dreamed, and he inherited everything. After the will was probated, he never opened the haberdashery again. He liquidated the assets and moved north to St. Louis. After a while he opened an exclusive shop for women in an area of exclusive shops, but before doing this he married a woman three years his senior, a Methodist from a good family. And always thereafter, for as long as he lived, the apostate felt like a traitor and carried within himself an unrelieved burden of guilt and a quiet conviction of his irrevocable damnation.

The marriage was not successful. He bought a fine house in a restricted residential area where every property had enough ground to insure reasonable privacy, and he tried very hard in every way that he could; but in spite of all his efforts the marriage went sour, and the truth was that it had no chance from the beginning. It was honestly not his fault, but his wife's.

A neurotic, she accumulated over a period of years an incredible number of psychosomatic ills; and it was not long before she decided that the state of her health made it imperative for her to deny her husband access to her body. She moved into a separate bedroom, and since she had never achieved a climax in her life, she was not aware of any personal loss in the discontinuance of a rather untidy function that she had always considered a disagreeable duty.

This was not true, however, with Aaron. His needs were normal and demanded satisfaction. He was a reasonably attractive man with more money than most men ever get; he could have had affairs, of course, or taken a permanent mistress, but he did not wish to risk emotional involvment or the possible development of an unfortunate situation. As an inadequate compromise, he went twice a month to a fashionable whorehouse on the south side of the city.

There was quite a bit of the moralist in him, and the biweekly trips to the south side disturbed his conscience some, adding to the burden of guilt that he already carried for other reasons. Because he was forced into them by his wife's abstinence, he came to look upon her as a source of corruption as well as a kind of parasite, and he hated her covertly and quietly. There was a short time when he considered rather academically the possibility of killing her and getting away with it, but of course his considerations came to nothing because he was really far too gentle to resort to violence and far too tender to the probings of his conscience to survive indefinitely as a murderer even if he could evade the retribution prescribed by law. Compensation for the deficiency of his marriage he found to a degree in his shop, and eventually to a greater degree in the young woman who came to work in the shop.

The shop prospered, though his marriage did not. He planned it himself from the beginning, specifying his choice of colors and fabrics and carpeting, and he had a genius for devising combinations of qualities that gave the effect of luxury without losing the aesthetic values of simplicity. His sense of what women would like, or ought to like and could be persuaded to like, was uncannily delicate and accurate. He displayed nothing but fine gowns, and he built quite rapidly a reputation which enticed the patronage of women who could afford to pay for both the gowns and his judgment in selecting them. But what he wanted more than anything else, and what he could not for a long time find the means of securing, was a selection of originals, originals in his own shop, which would compare favorably with the originals of New York and Paris. With these he could seduce and retain the patronage of women like Harriet Tyler who now selected most of their more expensive gowns in the shops of New York, at least, if not Paris.

While he was thinking of this and wondering how he could accomplish it, at the age of forty-five, he had his first heart attack. He was in the shop, fortunately in the back room supervising personally an alteration by the seamstress; and all of a sudden, without the slightest recognizable warning, he was overcome by the most terrible pain that he had ever known. A doctor was called by Gussie Ingram, his chief saleslady, and an ambulance was called by the doctor. The ambulance came into the alley behind the shop, and Aaron was carried out the rear exit on a stretcher. Mrs. Alton Sturdevant, who was at the time buying a hundred-and-fifty dollar cocktail gown in front, was never aware that anything had happened; and Aaron did not return for nearly two months.

This occurred in January, a month which Aaron's wife had begun to spend in Florida, and he did not find it necessary to inform her precisely what he had suffered. On her part, she did not find it any more necessary to return to find out. As a matter of fact, she was inclined to consider illness her special privilege, and she rather resented him as a trespasser. Not that he cared at all. He no longer wished to kill her, or even that she would die, for it would have been impossible for her to have been, really, any more dead to him than she already was.

He learned two things from his brush with death. The first was that his life to that point, in spite of the shop, had hardly been worth living. The second was that, nevertheless, he would rather go on living than die. For several months he exercised the excessive caution characteristic of heart-conscious persons; but as time passed and he suffered no new attack or any signs of one, he relaxed and lived more naturally, and began to think again about the originals. He even thought of trying to design them himself, but his talent was in judgment, not creation, and he knew that he would not be successful. Soon afterward, almost a year from the time of his attack, Donna Buchanan came to see him.

The first thing he noticed about her was that she was frightened and had adopted an air of excessive sophistication to disguise her fright. He noted this only briefly, however, because the second thing he noticed was that she was unusually attractive and had learned well the tricks of making herself look even more attractive than she naturally was. Her hair was black, but her skin was fair—and her lips were done boldly in vivid color. She was wearing a pair of harlequin glasses that increased the piquancy of her thin face. When she removed her heavy coat in response to his invitation, he saw that her body was fine and slim and good to look at; and he would have viewed it imaginatively in a number of his own gowns if he had not been so struck by the one she was wearing. It was a navy faille with the effective simplicity of fine design and the unmistakable clean lines of expensive tailoring.

"Excuse me," he said. "Where did you get that dress?"

"I made it," she said.

"Where did you get the pattern?"

"I designed it myself."

"Where did you learn to design?"

"I took a correspondence course, which helped, but mostly I've just worked at developing what I knew instinctively."

This was an answer that pleased him, for he had a great belief in feeling as the primary element of excellence in design, a kind of natural awareness of what was right and not right.

"Why have you come to see me?" he asked.

"To ask if you might have a place for me in your shop."

"As a designer?"

"I'd be willing to sell too, but I'd want to work part of the time on designing."

He nodded at the portfolio she had brought in with her.

"Are those some of your designs?"

"Yes."

"Show them to me."

She did, and his excitement increased. He knew at once that he was going to give her a place in his shop—there was no question about that from the very first—but he examined all the sketches without comment, visualizing their execution in this or that fabric, brocades and velvets and Jacquarded silks. Afterward he closed the portfolio and began to talk with her about conditions and terms as if it were quite simply understood by both of them that it was no more than a matter of clarifying the details of an arrangement that was inevitable.

She turned out to be not only a fine designer but also a subtle and effective saleslady; and even these assets, important as they were to the shop and its increasing distinction, were of minor significance as compared with her total effect in the life that Aaron had been living, less because he really wanted to live it than because he did not want to explore the consequences of dying. He soon loved her and wanted to possess her. This he confessed to himself, because he was painfully honest in the presence of his id, but he confessed it to no one else, certainly not to her, because he was considerate and shy and had no faith in his capacity to incite in her a reciprocal desire.

After a while she had her own key to the shop and often returned at night to work at her sketches, and sometimes, at the beginning, he was there himself when she came. Afterward he made a point of being there every time instead of only sometimes. For quite a long while he made a pretense of having his own late business in the shop, but then, abruptly, he abandoned the pretense entirely and spent all his time in the room where she worked. It gave him genuine pleasure merely to sit and watch her, and to talk with her when she wanted to talk, and even to feel within himself the aching carnal appetite that was now specifically dedicated for the first time in much too long. Because it was dedicated, because it was a part of love, it was therefore purified and no disturbance to his tender conscience.

One night when she was finished working, she turned and met his bitter-sad eyes and held them levelly with hers for the length of three long breaths.

"Are you in love with me?" she said.

Rather strangely, or perhaps not, he wasn't in the least disturbed by the question, and he answered that he was. "Would you like to have me?" she said. "Yes."

"Well, I think I would like to have you too, so why don't we try it and see how it works out?"

"Here? Now?"

"Do you object to here and now?"

"Oh, no. No."

"Well, then."

He was a little awkward the first time, and excessively gentle, but it worked out pleasantly for her, and wonderfully for him, and was repeated frequently afterward. She left home (she had been living with her mother and father) and rented an apartment, and he stayed with her there several nights a month. Or when his wife was out of town, they went to his house. He discontinued his trips to the south side. His life was suddenly warm and exciting, something it had never been before, and then, cataclysmically, in the midst of the warmth and excitement, about eight months after he took her the first time in the shop, he had his second heart attack.

He spent two months in the hospital and six weeks at home and was considered fortunate, by his doctor, to be alive. The shop in his absence was in Donna's charge. She visited him in the hospital and reported how things were going, and they went well. While he was convalescing at home, she did not see him at all, although she talked to him daily over the telephone, because she did not wish to meet the wife of the man with whom she had committed adultery and with whom she expected to commit it again. This was a reticence he could understand and approve of, but the six weeks at home were the longest of his life. He eventually escaped to the shop, and Donna, with vast relief, but always afterward he carried, or was supposed to carry, a supply of nitroglycerine tablets in his pocket.

Everything was resumed. Business and Donna and life. And the warmth and excitement were still there, the strong desire to live and do and be. It was never in him in greater force than it was the morning he awakened early, arose quietly, and looked down at her nakedness with love, and then descended the stairs of his house to drop dead in the hall in an instant.

3

Before she had walked from the house to the street, her feet were wet and very cold. She turned left at the street and walked directly down it for several blocks, looking right and left at each intersection for a drugstore or café or any establishment at all that might be open on a Sunday and have a telephone. At last she saw to her left, at an intersection, the unlighted neon identification of a drugstore.

While she felt for Aaron a genuine grief, it was not unmixed grief, and she felt also for herself a concern which had been expressed first in flight and would from this time on be expressed in a calculated effort to avoid implication. There was no real harm in this, of course—it was better for him as it was for her—but it entailed problems; and the most imperative of the problems was arranging that his body be found soon. This was a problem which could surely be solved simply, however, once she was in a position to think about it clearly, and, meanwhile, she wondered if anyone had seen her leave the house fifteen or twenty minutes ago. She doubted it, but even so, there were her footprints in the snow. She hoped the heavy snow would continue, and obliterate the prints.

She reached the drugstore and went to the telephone booth and dialed the number of a taxi company. When she started to give the address, she could not for a moment think of what it was, and she felt an odd, exorbitant panic out of all proportion to its cause, but then she remembered and provided with an equally disproportionate sense of relief the names of the two streets intersecting outside. Leaving the booth, she went up to the front entrance of the store to wait; and the taxi must have been cruising quite near when it received the radio message, for it was sounding its horn at the curb within four minutes. She went out and got in and gave the driver the address of the shop downtown.

Because of the heavily falling snow and the increasingly hazardous condition of the streets, it took an unusually long time to get there. Now that she was in the taxi, however, she lost much of her earlier sense of urgency and was acquiring in its place a feeling of apathy and a collateral inability to think of anything whatever constructively. Besides, she was becoming sleepy. She leaned back in the seat and closed her eyes and longed and longed to go to sleep.

When the taxi eventually stopped, she paid the fare and went directly through the shop to her workroom in the rear. Removing her coat and shoes and stockings, she rubbed her feet with a towel from the lavatory until warmth was restored to them, and then she removed the crimson sheath and put on dry stockings and the shoes and dress she had worn to work the day before. This done, she began to think in spite of herself in a way that she did not wish to think. Here in the shop that had been Aaron's, she was acutely susceptible to the sense of his presence, as if he were actually sitting and watching her with the bitter-sad light of his desire in his eyes; and her conviction of guilt and cowardice was intense and no longer evadable. She had come here and found first a friend and then a lover, if not complete love, and most of all she had found support in doing what she wanted most to do. Now the man who had received her and accepted her, the friend and lover, was lying dead beyond possible help, and she had run away from him when she might have stayed, had denied him when she might have given recognition and dignity to his body in death. Oh, she was a coward, she could not deny it, and perhaps she was even committing some crime, but still it was better, it was surely much better—if she could only achieve this conviction—to have done what she had done and would certainly continue doing.

She always came back to this. That it was better this way for him and for her. For herself, there was too much in precarious balance, too much to lose that had been gained, for there was no way of predicting the ramifications and effects of adultery and death in collusion. For him, there was little left to lose, but he would surely be grateful, if he could ever again be anything, that she had prevented the scandal. She knew that all this might be rationalization, but it worked to the point of leavening her guilt, and pretty soon she began to think about going home.

She did not want to go. She would have much preferred going to her own apartment, but it was necessary now to go home instead, not only because she felt committed to her mother for a part of each Sunday, but also because she needed her parents' help. She wanted them to be prepared to swear she had been home last night in case it was necessary or desirable for some reason she could not foresee.

She always thought of it as home, though it had never been that to her in any significant sense of the word; she had hated it while she was there, and had left it with relief. She dreaded going back even for a visit to the ugly, narrow two-story house cramped darkly between houses as high and ugly and narrow on either side.

She dreaded also seeing her mother and father. For her mother, she felt pity and some respect and a nagging sense of responsibility. For her father, a querulous ineffectual person who persisted ridiculously in trying to exercise the prerogatives of his position, without ever having assumed adequately the obligations, she felt contempt only. She wished she had never known him, would have liked never to see him again, and would surely never have gone near him or permitted him to come near her if it had not been for her mother.

When she was given a place in Aaron's shop, she began to plan immediately to move into an apartment, and she executed the plan a few days after the night Aaron took her in the back room. She still contributed money, however, to supplement her father's irregular income, always handing it directly to her mother, for whom she intended it and without whom she would not have given it. She visited the narrow, ugly house almost every Sunday, again for the sake of her mother only. Now she had to leave the shop and visit it again, this time, though, for her own sake too. It would be well, she thought, to go at once.

She did not call a taxi by telephone. She went through the shop to the front door and pulled the blind away from the glass a few inches and stood peering up the street until a taxi came into view. Then she went out quickly to the curb and stopped it and got in.

She began to wonder what would be the best way to get from her mother and father the consent to the lie that might never become necessary at all, but she could formulate no particular strategy, and probably would need none, for her mother was weak and her father was vulnerable. In the end they would simply do as she told them to. The taxi moved slowly through cloudy streets, and for a long while she sat erect in the back seat, looking through the taxi window at the changing character of the city as the buildings diminished and admitted the sky and became residential in allotments of blanketed lawn between shopping-center breaks. Then, when they moved at last into the mean streets of her earliest remembrance, she leaned back and closed her eyes and quit looking at anything at all except the tenacious image—of Aaron dead—behind her lids.

The taxi stopped in front of the narrow and ugly house. She opened her eyes, got out and overpaid the driver, and then went quickly up the stairs and across the high porch and into a dark hall. She paused in the hall to hang her coat on a rack fastened to the wall, and wondered with mounting depression why the smell never changed, never, never changed—the thin perennial and faintly sour smell which apparently had nothing to do with ventilation, or the lack of it, and was perhaps the breath of the house itself or the scent of sour lives. She turned away from the rack and started across to the entrance to the living room, and the voice of her mother came out to meet her. "Is that you, Donna?"

She answered that it was and went on into the room. Her mother was sitting in an overstuffed chair around which were scattered the several sections of a Sunday newspaper. She had been on the point of rising, but now she sank back and folded her hands in her lap and automatically tilted her head and turned her cheek for the swift kiss routinely accorded by this sleek and sometimes disturbing young woman who was (rather incredibly, she often thought) her daughter.

"Did you have trouble getting here?" she said.

"Because of the snow? No. None at all."

"I was worried. I thought you might have trouble, or might not be able to come at all."

"Well, I didn't, but I imagine it would be wise if I started back early."

"That's too bad. I see you so seldom."

"Once a week isn't so seldom, Mother."

"I wish you would live at home. It isn't right for a girl to be living alone in an apartment when she has a home to live in."

"Now, Mother, for Christ's sake, let's not start that all over again the moment I get here."

"I just can't help thinking I must have failed you some way. Why would a girl want to leave her home if she was happy in it?"

"I wasn't happy in it. I was damn miserable in it, as you know very well, but I've told you and told you that it wasn't your fault. If it hadn't been for you, I'd have gone long before I did. We've been over and over this, Mother, and I absolutely won't discuss it again, so let's please drop it right now or I'll leave."

She looked at her mother's face and quickly away, for she could never look at her long without ambivalence. It made her feel at once sad and contemptuous, and the reason was that her mother had been a beautiful woman and had not deserved to be. How in God's name could a woman who had been beautiful and reasonably intelligent have made such a drab mess of her life? And the most depressing thing of all was that her mother was not actually aware of the mess. She had been beautiful and intelligent, and she had wasted all of what she had been on a ridiculous ineffective who should have been discarded ages ago, and this depressing and senseless waste had happened simply because she was totally incapable of facing the truth about anything, because she had no guts, and she damn well deserved the consequences of not having any.

"I wish you wouldn't be so cross, dear," her mother said. "And that reminds me. I've been wanting to speak to you about your father. I know he's very irritating to you, but do you think you could just try a little harder to get along with him?"

"All Father has to do to get along with me is to mind his own damn business."

"Well, that's just what I mean. Don't you see, dear, that Father considers that you *are* his business? He only tries to think of what is good for you."

"Oh, hell. That kind of talk makes me sick. Whatever in my life has been done for my good has been done by you, or I have done it for myself. The truth is that Father has been a damn detriment to both of us, and you know it, and he has never done a thing that entitles him to any authority at all in my affairs. I tell you I don't wish to talk about him any more, now or ever, and if you don't stop dragging him up every time I'm here, I swear to God I'll leave and never come back."

"All right, dear, all right. I don't want to make you angry."

"Damn it to hell, I am not angry."

"Do you have to swear so much?"

"I'm sorry. The truth is, something has happened that worries me."

"Are you in trouble?"

"No. Not exactly. At least, I don't think so. Where's Father now?"

"Why, I was just going to tell you, dear. He's not at home. Only last week he took this selling job that keeps him out of town part of the time."

"You mean he wasn't home last night?"

"No, dear. He's been gone since last Thursday. He'll be back tomorrow, I think, if you want to see him."

"I don't want to see him. I'm just glad he wasn't here last night."

"That's a strange thing to say about your father, dear. Why are you glad?"

"Because I want you to promise to do something for me, and it will be better if he doesn't know anything about it. If I ask you to do something for me that may seem rather strange, will you do it?"

"Of course, dear. If I can. You know I always try to do anything for you that I can."

"I know, Mother. You've always been very good to me. It's really not so much to ask, after all. I only want you to promise to say that I spent last night here if anyone should ask you."

"To lie, dear? Why ever should you want me to do that?"

"Well, let's not get heavy about the lying, Mother. Chances are you won't have to say anything at all, but if you should, I want you to say that I was here. Will you do it?"

"I don't know. I don't like to tell lies unless it's absolutely necessary. You will have to tell me why you want me to say you were here when you really weren't."

Donna lit a cigarette and sat looking at her mother through the thin smoke between them. She had thought that it might be possible to arrange things without a confession, but now she saw that it wouldn't. Besides, she felt suddenly a rather perverse desire to be perfectly honest, not so much for the sake of honesty as for the sake of honesty's capacity to shock and disturb.

"Aaron's dead," she said.

"Aaron? Mr. Burns? The Aaron Burns you work for?"

"That's right. He died in his home last night, or perhaps early this morning, and that's why I want you to say I was here. It might ruin me if I were to become involved, and at the very least it would be unpleasant."

"Involved? I don't understand what you mean by becoming involved. For God's sake, you didn't have anything to do with his death, did you?"

"Oh God, Mother, will you please stop being so tragic? I already have enough to bear without this in addition. I didn't kill him, if that's what you mean, and I didn't contribute to his death indirectly, either. He had a heart condition. He simply died some time while I was asleep. Sometime in the night or early morning."

"You spent the night with him?"

"Yes. I have spent many nights with him."

"Oh, Donna, Donna! So your father was right after all! Sleeping with a married man, living like a—"

"Stop it, Mother! Stop it immediately! And if you say anything against Aaron, one damn word, I'll never speak to you again. Do you understand? He was kind and generous and gentle, which I am not and can never be, and we were good for each other. You needn't expect me to be ashamed of anything I have done. Do you think I will feel like a criminal because I committed adultery? Well, there was something between us that was what we both needed, and whatever it was, it was good. And I will tell you that it was infinitely more moral, if you are concerned about my morals, than the sour cohabitation that you and Father have been engaged in for as long as I can remember."

She had not intended to be so cruel, and she regretted at once that she had been. Sucking smoke into her lungs, she expelled it with a long exhalation and watched the slow crumbling and complete dissolution of the vestiges of beauty in her mother's face.

"Don't cry," she said. "Damn it to hell, please don't cry."

Standing up abruptly, sickened by ambivalence, she walked out of the living room and through the dining room into the kitchen. On the range was an aluminum pot half full of cold coffee. Lighting the burner under the pot, she stood watching it while the coffee heated. As she stood and watched she began to think with clarity of her position and all that stood in the balance now that Aaron was dead. Here in the ugly house she loathed, in the smell and the shadow of the life she had escaped, she was morbidly aware of what she stood to lose, the shop and her job and all that they entailed and promised. It was not fair after she had schemed and worked so long and so hard, it was simply the rottenest piece of goddamn luck at just the time when everything was going so beautifully. Suddenly, to Aaron, wherever he was, her mind cried out a thin, irrational indictment of betrayal.

Why did you have to die? she thought. *Oh, why in hell did you have to die?*

CHAPTER II

One of Donna's earliest recollections in the area of inceptive light, where remembrance survived in scattered oddments, was the sound of a sewing machine. In the beginning there was one kind of sound, and a little later there was a slightly different kind of sound, and this change occurred when her mother's old treadle-driven machine was traded in for one with an electric motor. She was sorry to see the old machine go, for the treadle had fascinated her, and she had become quite proficient at working it with her hands while sitting on the floor and looking across under the golden oak cabinet at her mother's knees. Her mother was glad to be thus relieved of the labor of pumping, and it was pleasant on the floor with her head full of the incisive sound, and the bright fabrics sometimes tumbling over the edge of the machine and behind her to form a kind of silk or cotton or warm wool tent. The old machine was a Bartlett and the new one was a Singer. She remembered the name of the old one quite clearly because it was spelled out in iron letters between iron legs in a shallow arc that served as a brace. The name was also spelled out on the treadle, which consisted of a kind of intricate filigree around the name inside a rectangular iron frame.

A significant oddment was Mrs. Kullen. Mrs. Kullen's husband was a meat cutter who had acquired his own market, and one of the benefits deriving from her marriage to this prosperous merchant was solvency sufficient for the hiring of a seamstress to modify her fat butt. There were other women who came to the cramped and narrow house for fittings, and some of them were even remembered for a while after they ceased to come, but it was Mrs. Kullen who became and remained the gross symbol of oppression, the prototype in Donna's mind of those who become dominant through a distortion of values.

Her mother was then beautiful, and employed a fine talent, and those who came to her should have come for favor and not for service, but this was not so. It was perfectly apparent that her mother was considered by these dull and demanding women to be little more than a menial, and it was her mother's fault, because she was weak and submissive and did not know how to utilize her own superiority. And it was in Donna the beginning of the ambivalence on the one hand, toward her mother, and concentrated contempt on the other, toward all of those for whom Mrs. Kullen stood. And Mrs. Kullen stood for them in her corset. She stood in the room in a slant of sun among a myriad of particles of suspended dust, and the angle of the narrow band of light fell across her fat white downy thighs between her corset and her stockings. This was Donna's first sight of her, or at least the sight which assumed precedence over all others in time and intensity, and it was the way, the only way, she was ever able to see her afterward in her mind.

For quite a while she seemed to share the house only with her mother and the machine and occasionally the women who came for fittings, and then all of a sudden, emerging from darkness as if he had been gone since her birth and had just returned, there was Wayne Buchanan, her father. It was not true that he had been gone, of course. He was there all the time from the beginning, but for some reason that she could not determine he was excluded from her earlier recollections. Neither could she determine why it was that he took his place so abruptly at the time that he did, but he must have been brought into focus by something unpleasant, something now forgotten that he said or did, for he took shape in an animus that was never overcome. Surely she had formerly felt some affection for him, or had accepted him at least with a kind of tolerance, but the feeling was extinct, if it had existed at all, before it had left a trace in her mind.

Wayne Buchanan was a tall man with heavy shoulders, handsome in a rather florid fashion. Later, when Donna was studying history in school, she thought that he actually resembled the Buchanan who had been fifteenth President of the United States, and this was ironic, besides being a coincidence of names and appearance, because the other Buchanan had been weak and a failure too. He had been, however, a failure on a high level, which was one thing, while Wayne Buchanan was a failure on a low level, which was quite another. He had somehow decided that selling was the thing he did best, and he was always leaving one job for another which promised to be better. But the promise was never kept, and he accomplished so many minor failures in such rapid succession that they seemed to combine in retrospect into one big indivisible failure together, which was really what they amounted to. Not that he looked or acted like the failure he was. His appearance remained impressive, and he supported his natural weakness with a rigidity of attitude that obscured the weakness as it supported it, and it was this rigidity that prevented him from disintegrating entirely.

He was known as a religious man. He said grace at the table and took his wife and daughter every Sunday to church, and because he had no confidence in his own moral stamina, he was particularly critical of the morals of others, and wished to impose upon them dogmas of belief and behavior that they did not wish to adopt for themselves. Donna did not object to grace or church, the truth being that she rather enjoyed these things for the comfortable feeling that they gave her for a short time afterward, nor did she object strenuously to continual admonitions to be a good girl, for she had no active intention of being anything else. What she objected to and despised was her father's propensity for making formulistic goodness a substitute for genuine devotion and for the capacity to do anything whatever that amounted to a damn. She understood with a kind of childish insight that a person who does not feel himself successful has much to gain from believing himself good, and she might have tolerated this in a more casual relationship. But she could not tolerate it in a relationship which was supposed to invoke respect, if not love, and she never did.

Besides being basically a fraud, Wayne Buchanan was something of a sadist. In a petty way, of course, as was appropriate for a weak man. He enjoyed denying Donna the things she could have had, and he enjoyed prohibiting her things she could have done. Many things were denied her, it was true, because Buchanan never had very much money and simply could not afford to supply them, and this was a valid reason for denial that Donna would have accepted if it had ever been offered, but it wasn't. Buchanan was constitutionally incapable of making such a simple admission, for it would have seemed to him a confession of impotence. His denials were always accompanied by some pompous hocus-pocus intended to make Donna believe that they were for her own benefit, as if not having whatever she wanted was necessarily good for her character, while having it would necessarily be bad. His phoniness in this respect was clearly evident, even to a child, and as she grew older—Donna the girl becoming Donna the woman—she learned to avoid the revolting routine by asking him at first for nothing she wanted and, a little later, by honestly not wanting anything he had to give.

Although she did not have as much as many children have when they are growing up, she always had, because of her mother's talent and trade, all the pretty dresses that she could wear, and this was very important to a pretty girl. Her mother bought fabric at a remnant shop for a fraction of its regular cost, but it was good material that was only marked down because it was the last of a bolt or dye lot or of a pattern that was being discontinued. On Donna the finished dresses her mother made had a look of quality that more expensive dresses did not have on other girls. In the beginning, that is, the material was bought and the dresses made by the mother for the daughter, but after a while the buying and the making were done by the daughter for herself, who had, besides her mother's skill with the machine, a better eye for color and its ultimate effect in design, and, most of all, a sure feeling for the design itself—whether it was right or wrong and why. Long before she took her correspondence course, she was making sketches in a cheap tablet and cutting patterns from newspapers.

Being pretty, and wearing with a flair her pretty dresses, she was attractive to boys, but she wasn't particularly popular. There is a legitimate distinction here, of course—and if she was glad of the one, she was undisturbed by the other, for the truth was that boys interested her mildly but not excessively, and she had not yet reached the point where she found them useful.

Her first intimate experience was with a quite small boy, when she herself was quite small, and it didn't amount to much. He was called Dinky, and he lived for a while with his father and mother and six brothers and sisters in a house three doors away. She played with him sometimes in her back yard or his, and one day they went down into the cellar under his house and explored each other's areas of difference with curiosity. It seemed a natural enough thing to do, and not too disappointing on the whole. She probably would have been willing to repeat the performance if circumstances had fallen out right for it, but unfortunately Dinky's family was dispossessed within the week for nonpayment of rent, and he moved away with his father and mother and six brothers and sisters, and she never saw him again. She thought about him for a while, but she didn't miss him. Once she tried to remember his last name and couldn't, and this caused her to wonder if she had actually ever known it, but she couldn't remember that either.

After Dinky, who hardly counted, she grew older, and she knew other boys who also hardly counted, and then when she was fifteen and had not yet decided what kind of person she wanted to be—or rather had not become aware of the kind of person she had to be—there was a boy named David who counted very much and was always remembered and regretted, not for what he was or had or did, but simply because he became an issue over which her father made a fool of himself and of her in the most disgusting way.

She went with this boy to what was called a formal dance—formal meant only that the girls wore long gowns and the boys wore the best they had, whatever that was. The dance was held in the gymnasium of the high school, and Donna wasn't especially eager to go, but when this boy named David asked her, she decided that she would. He was a handsome boy with light curly hair—but he was not so conceited as many boys who thought they were exceptional merely because they were good-looking—and he was in love with her at the time, though she was not in love with him. His being in love with her made her feel important and fairly responsive.

It was quite a distance from her home to the high school, but they walked there, having no other way of getting there, and after the dance was over at eleven-thirty, they walked home. It was a warm May night with the softest stirring of air, and it was pleasant and exciting walking along the streets together, and she was glad when he took her hand and held it as they walked.

They reached her house about midnight, and sat down together on the edge of the high porch with their feet on the steps below them, and it was different at that time in the ugly neighborhood from what it had ever been or would ever be again, an illusion in the light of stars and moon of grace and quietude. He told her awkwardly that he loved her and asked her if she loved him in return, and she said that she did for his sake and the illusion's, although she knew with a strange and aching sadness that it was not true, that she was really in love with half an hour of a May night and with herself in that fragment of time. In response to her lie, he put his arms around her and kissed her, and she found it agreeable. When he did it again, she responded by putting her arms around him also, and felt one small breast cupped gently in a hand, and heard behind them in that instant the explosive opening of the screen door.

It was her father who came out, who had certainly crept downstairs to spy on them, and he was in such a fury that she thought for a minute he had gone crazy. He jerked David to his feet before the boy had time to defend himself. Slapping him three times in the face with all his strength, her father gave him such a violent shove that the boy lost his balance on the steps and fell sprawling on the walk below. All this, Wayne Buchanan did to the boy Donna had almost loved in a graceful fragment of time.

On the sidewalk, David got to his feet and began to sob, not so much in fear or pain as in anger of his own.

"You son-of-a-bitch," he said. "You mean son-of-a-bitch."

Wayne Buchanan started down the steps, and the boy turned and ran, and Buchanan also turned and came back up onto the porch.

"Go upstairs to your room," he said.

She looked at him levelly, and she was not really angry nor in the least afraid. If he had been a stranger, she might have felt fear or anger or possibly both, but he was not a stranger, he was her father, and she was only sickened and shamed and ineffably lost.

"You heard what he called you," she said. "He called you a mean son-of-a-bitch, and that's what you are. You're a mean, dirty son-of-a-bitch of a hypocrite, and I wish you were dead. I hope David comes back with a gun and shoots you dead."

He raised a heavy hand and struck her in the face. Her light body was slammed back by the blow against the siding of the house, and she slipped down slowly into a sitting position with the long, full skirt of her new gown billowing around her like a bright cloud. A thin, bitter fluid came up from her stomach into her mouth, and she thought for a terrible moment that she was going to vomit, which would have been, somehow, the most shameful thing of all, and then she stood up and faced him again.

"Don't ever hit me again," she said. "Don't hit me or touch me so long as you live."

Turning away from him, she opened the screen door and went into the house quietly, and in the end, in a monstrous perversion of normal effect, it was he who was afraid.

2

It was not the first time he had been afraid. As a boy, he was afraid of his father, who was a minister of the gospel, and later on, when he was himself studying for the ministry at a small denominational college, he was afraid in a different kind of way of a young man named Cletus Corey, who was his roommate.

Cletus Corey was known as a rather dangerous liberal among the three or four hundred students in the college. It was his theory that a minister of the gospel, in order to be really effective, should have a rich, empirical knowledge of the world and its works, even at the expense of minor virtues, and he was fond of pointing out that even Saint Francis of Assisi had been quite a rounder in his younger years. This theory of deliberate deviation for the sake of worldly effectiveness was disturbing enough in itself, but it was made doubly so by illustrative use of the saint, who had been a Catholic (Roman), of course, and was therefore not an acceptable example for young Christians living in the age of enlightenment. But Cletus was certainly *catholic* (meaning liberal) and he looked to all sorts and extremes of examples in the application of his theory to himself. He was able to admire both William Jennings Bryan and Clarence Darrow. He subscribed to the *American Mercury,* read H. L. Mencken with roars of delight, and passed *Elmer Gantry* around to his more liberal cronies. It was generally predicted that he would either be an enormous success or become an enormous cropper, but as it turned out, neither of these predictions was fulfilled. In time, at the request of the college authorities, he abandoned his theological studies, and shortly afterward, at the request of an impatient parent, he got a job and made quite a bit of money selling secondhand automobiles.

He left college at the same time that Wayne Buchanan left, and for the same reason. The truth is, the reason for their leaving was quite a scandal at the time, and it was all the unfortunate result of Cletus Corey's applied theory. The ingredients of the scandal were juicy and really deserved the attention of more accomplished practicioners than Buchanan and Corey. They included a roadhouse, a stripper, drunkenness, and fornication. The roadhouse was a notorious highway spot known as the Blue Barn, because it looked like a barn and was painted blue, and it was strictly off-limits to students of the college, but Corey had been there before without subsequent retribution, temporal or divine, and he kept suggesting to Buchanan that it would be broadening and beneficial if he were to go also.

"It's a kind of moral obligation to have some experience in these things," he said. "In my opinion, it's a pretty poor sort of minister who can't trust himself to find out what life's like just because he's afraid it will corrupt him."

This argument appealed to Buchanan. He saw himself standing strong and clean and unassailable, a source of salvation among the fleshpots.

"After all," Buchanan said, "what if the prophets had ignored Sodom and Gomorrah and Babylon and such places as that? It's perfectly apparent that the prophets knew all about them, and that's why they were able to combat their evil and even save some of the sinners who would otherwise have been lost in them."

"Now you're getting it," Corey said.

"What's this Blue Barn like?" Buchanan said.

"Well, it's just a big room with a bar and a lot of chairs and tables and a place to dance. There's a small band Saturday nights, and they have a floor show at eleven and another around one. They must pay off to the cops or something, because there's quite a lot of drinking and sometimes it gets pretty rough."

"What kind of floor show do they have?"

"There's this fellow introduces the acts, an M.C. he's called, and he sings some songs that are really pretty dirty and disgusting, and there are a couple of girls who dance."

"What kind of dance?"

"They just sort of move around to the music and make motions of various kinds and take off their clothes."

"No fooling? How do they get away with that sort of thing?"

"Oh, well, there's no law against it, so far as that goes."

"No temporal law, maybe."

"Sure, sure. I'm not saying it's right, you understand. One of these girls is called Trixie, and she's about as pretty as any girl you could see anywhere. It makes you feel real bad to see her dancing around practically naked in front of all those men and all. If the right fellow came along who could make her see how she shouldn't do things like that, he could probably save her."

"Well, that would certainly be commendable," Buchanan said. "We mustn't forget the parable of the black sheep."

"Nor Mary Magdalen either."

"That's true. That's certainly true."

This line of thought was also appealing to Buchanan. He considered himself a right fellow in any possible contingency, and now, considering the practically naked Trixie, he actually wondered if he might not be receiving some kind of call. He could see himself saving her from the shame of ogles, and in his imagination receiving her gratitude and love—platonic, of course, unless he went so far as marrying her for her own good, in which eventuality there were additional purifying possibilities as well as a satisfying element of sacrifice.

"I'll tell you what I'll do," he said. "I'll go out there with you next Saturday night just to see what it's like."

"That's the stuff. I got a friend downtown who'll let me use his car if he isn't going to be using it himself. I'll find out and let you know."

"All right. It's agreed, then, that we'll go just to see what it's like."

As it developed, the friend's car was available, and Buchanan and Corey drove out to the Blue Bam the next Saturday night on what was really, Buchanan kept telling himself, a kind of mission. Unfortunately, the management of the Blue Barn was not aware of their status as missionaries, which should have exempted them from certain obligations, and it was made clear to them at once that they would buy drinks or get out.

"It's all right," Corey said. "They're not very strong drinks, anyhow, and you can sort of nurse yours along."

What he didn't say, however, is that the strength of a drink is relative to the resistance of the drinker, and Buchanan, having had no practice, had practically no resistance. He tried to nurse the first drink according to instruction, but it was the policy of the management to serve fresh ones at fairly short intervals, with or without a specific order, and after a while it began to seem imperative for the sake of appearances to empty some of the glasses on the table in order to get them out of sight. This he set about doing with the assistance of Corey, but they never seemed quite to catch up, and when eleven o'clock came, time for the first show, he was considerably more vulnerable to the corruptions of his mission than it is safe for a missionary to be. The M.C. was truly a disgusting fellow with no claim on Christian charity, and the first dancer, billed as Nanette the Naughty, was only a mild threat to asceticism. But when Trixie came gliding into light to the roll of a drum in an ice-blue satin gown, it was for Buchanan, though he had it to learn, a triumph of flesh in an hour of ruin. She was a slim and sinuous temptress with short curly hair that was almost white, and she gave the impression of being little more than a physically precocious child. Actually, though this was something else that Buchanan did not know, she was fully ten years older than she looked and had never been a child at all. She filled him at sight with a flaming and holy desire, at once with a need to save her from her sordid life. By the time she had finished removing the ice-blue gown, he was committed to a farce and assured of his shame.

"What a rotten crime!" he said, panting a little with an emotion that had nothing to do with his expressed indignation.

"Crime?" Corey said, failing for the moment to readjust to a missionary status. "What's a crime?"

"Her dancing like that. A young, pretty girl like her in front of all these men."

"Oh, that. Well, yes, it is, of course. It's a downright crime."

"I must talk with her, Corey. I simply must."

"I don't know that I'd do it, if I were you, Buchanan. These girls are pretty expensive when you get to fooling around with them."

"What in heaven's name do you mean? Are you suggesting that I want to … to buy favors from this girl?"

"No, no. Not at all, Buchanan. I only mean that the management expects you to buy them drinks and all if they sit with you at a table."

"I don't intend for her to sit with me at a table. I must talk with her privately."

Corey, who was not exceptionally charitable and had read, besides, Somerset Maugham's story of Sadie Thompson, looked at Buchanan with a growing and perhaps excusable cynicism. Buchanan, who had not read the story or even seen Jeanne Eagles in the movie, was nevertheless sensitive to the look and its implications.

"Is it your opinion that I am basely motivated in this matter?" he said.

"To tell the truth," said Corey, getting directly to the point, "it's my opinion that you're drunk."

Which was true. Buchanan was quite drunk from trying to catch up, but he was also more than that. He was exhilarated and inviolable and filled with holy fire. Rising unsteadily, he looked down for a moment at Corey with imperious contempt, and then, without a word, he turned and made his precarious way among the tables toward the door through which Trixie had gone with a twitch of her rear in the completion of her act. Beyond the door was a short and narrow and dirty hall with an exit at the far end and four other doors spaced along it, two on each side, and in the hall, lounging indolently, was a man with incredible muscles inside a soiled white shirt.

"Where the hell you think you're going, sonny?" he said amiably.

Buchanan replied with dignity that he wanted to speak with Miss Trixie.

"I don't know, sonny," he said. "I'll see what she says."

He went back to one of the doors and knocked on it and talked through it and then returned to Buchanan.

"She says it's okay to come in, sonny," he said. "Have fun."

Buchanan, scorning to draw inference from implication, went to the door and also knocked.

"It's not locked, lover," a rather brassy voice said.

Trixie had risen from a worn red couch to welcome him, and the only change she had made in her costume since leaving the spotlight was to remove the last two ounces of wispy material from here and there. She had, of course, no way of knowing that Buchanan was a fool, and, proceeding on an assumption to which she was certainly entitled by circumstances, she was simply prepared to supplement her income as she had supplemented it many times before in the only way she knew that did not involve prolonged drudgery. Moreover, having other things to do before her one o'clock show, she did not intend to waste time. In brief, Buchanan was quite probably one of the weakest protagonists of light against darkness since the time of Zoroaster. Afterward, sobered and revolted and terrified by an instantaneous conviction of mortal sin, he wondered why he had not noticed earlier that her feet were dirty.

"Bitch," he said. "Dirty bitch."

She was speechless for a minute with astonishment and fury in succession, and then her voice returned with a hiss.

"What the hell's the matter with you? What kind of talk is that, I'd like to know. You come back here, you bastard, you get what you want, and then you call me names. Give me my money and get the hell out of here and don't ever come back."

"Bitch!" he said. "Bitch, bitch, bitch!"

She leaped at him and raked fingernails down his face, and he slashed back at her in a kind of blind hatred. She fell back on the couch and cursed and began to scream. Turning to escape, he ran into the arms of the muscled man of the hall, who began without delay to beat him without mercy. Agent of his corruption, witness to his humiliation, the Blue Barn Jezebel watched and laughed and cursed and jeered. Eventually, he was hauled to the door at the end of the hall and thrown out onto the ground. He lay for a minute or two without moving, tasting his blood in his mouth, and then he dragged himself to his feet and limped painfully around to the gravel parking area. Five minutes later Corey came out of the Blue Barn in a hurry and joined him.

"For God's sake, what did you do in there?"

Buchanan sobbed and shook his head and said nothing.

"Look," Corey said, "you've got to tell me what happened. Why did they want to know who we are and where we came from?"

Then Buchanan was really terrified.

"You didn't tell them!" he gasped. "Oh, God, you didn't tell them!"

"What would you have done with a big gorilla looking down your throat and threatening to tear you to pieces if you didn't?"

"Oh, God!" Buchanan sobbed. "Oh, merciful Christ!"

Later, in his room at the college, trying desperately to be rational about it, he decided that the management of the Blue Barn was certainly in no position to invite the attention of the authorities or the wrath of the college officials. As a matter of fact, the existence of the Blue Barn was precarious and could hardly have survived a charge of corrupting embryo ministers, but he failed to take into proper account the vindictiveness of Trixie. On

Monday a crudely spelled and printed note was received by the dean, and within the hour following, Buchanan was summoned and charged. Although he lied heroically, it was to no avail, for Corey in a separate session had told a conflicting story. Buchanan was flayed with Christian wrath and salted with Christian scorn, and he was sent smarting to his room to await the coming of his father.

He went to his room, all right, but he did not wait. He would rather have faced the devil himself than the man who had sired him. He left the college and caught a bus to St. Louis, and he never saw his father again until after the man was dead, at which time he went home to attend the funeral and collect five hundred dollars that had been left him in a final spirit of paternal charity. He worked at various jobs and was not very successful at any of them, and while he still had most of the five hundred dollars left, he married a very pretty young woman named Ellen Fischer. He married her and unconsciously hated her because she excited him sexually, thereby degrading him, and when they had a child about two years later, he unconsciously hated her also, because she would in her turn excite and degrade someone else.

3

Inasmuch as she was an attractive girl, she excited a good many boys, but it would be impossible to identify them. However, it would be possible to identify definitely the several who, on the other hand, excited her, and the first of these was a boy named Enos Simon.

She met him when she was a senior in high school, and she had by that time decided what she wanted to do and what kind of person she wanted to be. She had enrolled in a correspondence course in design, which she studied in addition to her regular school assignments, and she had definitely abandoned any idea of going to college. She would have liked to go, so far as that was concerned, but only if she could do it in a manner that suited her, which was out of the question for financial reasons. So she enrolled in the correspondence course as an alternative, and she worked very hard at it, and at the same time she began deliberately to try to achieve a certain effect physically. She designed and made her clothing for the achievement of this, and she also became artful in the use of cosmetics. It was in this period, just before she met Enos Simon, that she went to the optometrist and bought the harlequin glasses.

She met Enos in the reading room of a branch library about a mile from her home. The task of carrying the correspondence course and doing well at the same time in her school work was proving rather strenuous, and she had acquired the habit of going directly from school to the library in order to accomplish as much as possible before going home. The day she first saw

Enos there, she was sitting as usual at a large table at which as many as six people could be seated, and he moved slowly across in front of her, beyond the table along a tier of shelves against a wall. He seemed to be reading titles in a rather desultory way, not stopping to remove and open any of the books, and what struck her at very first sight was an air of somber intensity about him. His skin was swarthy, his hair was dark and tumbled and slightly curly, and although he was clean he was somewhat unkempt, as if he had a fine indifference to the effect of his clothes, which had in its own way its own effect. He carried his head tilted a little forward, his chin tucked down, and this gave him the appearance of looking up at an angle under his heavy brows with a kind of repelling expression, not so much of belligerence as of a fierce desire to be let alone. He drifted along the tier of shelves and out of sight without stopping or looking once in Donna's direction, but she thought of him that night and looked for him when she returned the next afternoon.

He was there, sitting alone at the very same table she had sat at yesterday, and she was shaken by the strong feeling she had upon seeing him. It was as if his presence were something she had planned, and it amounted, therefore, to a conquest.

He was slouched in his chair with his legs extended under the table, and when she sat down across from him, she accidentally kicked one of his feet. He drew the foot away and looked up at her from his book with that oddly fierce expression she had noticed before.

"Excuse me," she said.

He grunted and lowered his eyes, but she continued to stare across at him as she opened the chemistry text she intended to study, and after a while he looked up again to meet her gaze.

"I wish you wouldn't stare at me," he said.

"Why? Do you feel guilty?"

"Guilty? Why the devil should I feel guilty?"

"Because you have such bad manners."

"What do you know about my manners? You know nothing about them at all."

"I know that you stick your legs out in all directions, which is rude, and I know that you haven't even the courtesy to acknowledge an apology."

"All right. Now you have told me off, and you can quit staring at me."

"I am just wondering why you never comb your hair."

"So now we are being rude to each other! It's a pleasure to tell you that my hair, and what I do or don't do to it, is none of your damn business."

"Perhaps not. But it's rather fascinating just the same. Rather like Raggedy Andy's. Like a string mop. I'm also wondering why you let your clothes get to looking as if you slept in them. Is it a kind of pose or something?"

"Suppose it is. You're something of a poseur yourself, aren't you? Why do you wear glasses shaped like that, for instance, and why do you fix your face and your hair to make you look like a college girl at least, when you're obviously only in high school?"

"Do my looks offend you?"

"Not at all. I don't care what you try to look like."

They had started talking in whispers, but their voices had risen in the exchange, and suddenly a female librarian appeared from around a tier of shelves and hissed at them sharply. The boy turned his head indolently in her direction and hissed back at her deliberately.

"Old crow," he said.

The librarian flushed and wagged an admonishing finger and retreated.

"My God," Donna whispered, "there's no *end* to your bad manners, is there?"

"I don't like being hissed at," he said.

"Well, neither do I, so we had better stop talking."

"Must we? Now that you've started it, I'm not sure that I want to stop."

"Don't I have anything to say about it?"

"Oh, I suppose I'd eventually get tired and quit talking if you simply refused to listen or make any reply."

"Yes, but before that happened, you might get thrown out of here."

"That's true. And you might get thrown out also, since you're involved. Would you feel humiliated if you were?"

"I think I'd manage to survive."

"I'm sure you would. But it seems silly to invite trouble. There are lots of places we could talk all we wanted to."

"What places?"

"I don't know. Lots of them."

"Are you asking me to leave with you?"

"Not yet. I'll ask you, though, if you promise to agree. I don't like being rejected."

"That's two things you don't like. Being hissed at and being rejected."

"There are others. Many others. Do you agree to go?"

"Yes."

"Then I ask you to leave with me."

They closed their books and stood up and went out past the desk of the angry librarian, and outside they stood on the sidewalk that was wet from an earlier rain and wondered where they should go together in the soft mid-May afternoon that was almost evening.

"If we are going some place together," she said, "we should at least know each other's name. Mine's Donna Buchanan."

"Mine's Enos Simon. Where would you like to go?"

"I don't know. Why don't you just choose one of the lots of places you know about?"

"Do you like beer?"

"I've never drunk any."

"I knew that look of yours was phony."

"What look?"

"You try to make people think you're a lot more experienced than you really are."

"Oh, hell. The truth is, you talk pretty silly sometimes, do you know that? I was eighteen this month, as a matter of fact, and that's as old as I care to be or look at present. Besides, what has not drinking beer got to do with anything? Do you measure experience by such silliness?"

"Never mind. It's not important, and I don't want to argue about it. I suggest that we walk down to Sully's and have a sandwich and a cup of coffee. Are you hungry?"

"Yes. I think I'd like a sandwich."

"All right. Have you been to Sully's?"

"No."

"It's not much."

He took her books, and they walked the six blocks on the wet sidewalk to Sully's. As Enos had said, it wasn't much of a place. The booths ran down one wall, and the counter ran down the other, and between the booths and the counter were a few tables. At the rear of the room was a jukebox with colored bubbles rising and descending soundlessly in lighted tubes. They sat and listened to the music until the man had returned with their order and gone again and the box was silent.

"Now that we're here and free to talk without being hissed at," Donna said, "what shall we talk about?"

"You can start by telling me why you kicked me in the library and then picked a quarrel with me."

"I kicked you quite by accident, and I did not pick a quarrel with you. You were rude, and I told you so, that's all. Please don't be so vain as to think I kicked you on purpose just to get your attention."

"Well, didn't you?"

"Of course not. You were sprawled all over the place."

"Oh, all right. I'll be more honest than you and admit that I've noticed you in the library before. I was trying to think of a way to meet you when it happened."

"You certainly didn't sound as if you wanted to meet me."

"That's just my way. The truth is, I'm shy and get all tensed up in such circumstances. Did you say you go to high school?"

"You said it, not I. But it's true. I'm a senior. I'll graduate next month."

"Are you going to college in the fall?"

"No."

"Why not?"

"Because I don't want to. There's something else I'd rather do."

"Get married?"

"God, no! I want to be a designer. A fashion designer. I'm taking a correspondence course in design now, but I don't think it's much help. The main thing is, I seem to have a natural talent for it."

"Did you design the dress you're wearing?"

"Yes. I designed it and made it."

"I agree that you have a talent. Can you get very far with something like fashion designing in St. Louis? I should think you'd have to go somewhere like New York."

"If you had an exclusive shop to work through, you could go a long way right here. That's what I'm going to try to do when I get good enough. I'm going to try to start a line of originals in a shop right here."

"You're very ambitious, aren't you?"

"I guess so. Aren't you?"

"No. I can't even make up my mind what I want to do."

"What do you mean, you can't make up your mind? Don't you do anything now?"

"No. I graduated from high school a year ago, and I haven't done anything since."

"Really? Nothing at all?"

"Not a damn thing. I've been thinking about it, but I can't seem to get started. I'm going to the state university this fall, but it's more because my old man thinks I ought to than because I really want to."

"Isn't there anything at all you think you'd like to do?"

"Well, I think I'd like to be a writer, but I'm sure I could never be anything but a poor one, so I guess I won't even try. Maybe I'll end up teaching."

"What would you teach?"

"Oh, literature. Something like that."

"Do you like to read?"

"I read a lot. Always have. It's the only thing I do much of."

She nodded at the book he had carried with hers from the library.

"What are you reading now?"

"The *Grand Testament.*"

"The Bible, you mean?"

"Lord, no! Villon's *Grand Testament.*"

"Who's Villon?"

"Seriously? Don't you actually know? How can you be so ignorant?"

"Well, you needn't start being insulting and rude again. If you do, I'll leave. I guess there are a few things I know that *you* don't, as far as that goes."

"That's true. I have a nasty way of thinking the only things worth knowing are the things I happen to know myself."

"That's better. You can be very nice when you want to be. Will you tell me who this Villon is? Is he French? His name sounds French."

"You're right except for your tense. Was, not is. He was born in Paris in 1431 and disappeared in 1463. No one knows what happened to him after that, but probably he was hanged."

"Why on earth do you think he was probably hanged?"

"Because he had almost been hanged two or three times before, and it doesn't seem likely that he could go on escaping by the skin of his teeth forever. He was a murderer and a thief and a whoremonger and a syphilitic and almost anything bad you could mention, but he also happened to have a master's degree from the Sorbonne and to be the greatest poet of the Middle Ages, and one of the greatest poets of any age. Don't you think that's very amusing?"

"I admit that I don't see anything amusing about it at all."

"Don't you? I do. A common criminal who worshiped beauty and wrote some of the most beautiful poetry in the world in cheap taverns and whorehouses and prisons and all sorts of low places. He was a coward, too. He was afraid of physical pain, and he was especially afraid of dying, because he had lived such a sinful life that the mere thought of dying filled him with terror. A criminal and a coward who wrote all this beautiful poetry that's still read after more than five hundred years. Beauty and evil co-existing in such extremity in one ugly and diseased little man. Don't you see why I consider it amusing? It's so ironical and paradoxical, and it's so contrary to what all the good little mediocre people try to teach you about evil not begetting beauty, and all that kind of crap. Would you like to hear something he wrote?"

"I guess so."

"All right. Listen to this."

He began to recite *Ballad of Dead Ladies,* the Rossetti translation, and each time he repeated the sad refrain with which each stanza ended, his voice assumed an intensity that was very compelling, as if he were himself acutely aware of the brevity of life and was urging in her an equal awareness.

When he had finished, he was silent for a moment, looking at her intently across the table, and she didn't know what to say. Up to then, she had honestly considered him rather ridiculous, although interesting, but now she saw he had sensibilities she had not imagined, and she no longer considered him at all ridiculous. The truth was, he disturbed her a little, more than she was prepared to admit, and she began to think that it was time to go home.

"You're right," she said. "It is beautiful."

"Do you think so? It's probably the most famous thing he did. It's called *Ballad of Dead Ladies.*"

She had by this time finished her sandwich and coffee, and she slipped sidewise, on the red leather seat and stood up abruptly, impatient with herself for permitting him to affect her so strongly.

"I think I'd better go now," she said.

"All right." He also slipped out of the booth and stood up, lifting their books from the table. "Do you live far from here?"

"Not so far. It's about a mile, I think."

"Will you let me go with you? I haven't got any place to go, except home, and I would much rather walk along with you."

She was ashamed of the house and neighborhood in which she lived, but she was also proud and defiant, so she said he could. After that, they met several times a week in the branch library and went out together from there, and a little later they began seeing each other in the evenings. But they didn't go many places or do many things because there didn't seem to be anything Enos really cared about, quite apart from the fact that he was in bad at home for his indolence and was given little money to spend. The first significant thing about him that Donna learned was that it was impossible ever to anticipate his mood. Sometimes he was gay and really clever, other times he was sullen and difficult to get along with, and still at other times, in what seemed to be a kind of intermediate mood between the two extremes, he was quietly considerate, almost tender, and seemed to be making a kind of plea that was never quite clarified.

On the whole, he was much too disturbing in proportion to his appeal, and she thought more than once she would tell him she didn't care to see him again, but she never did. Their relationship continued past her graduation and into the summer nearing the time when he would have to go away to the university. Several times, at some propitious moment, it wavered briefly on the verge of demand and eager submission, but nothing was gained or lost. Then he came the evening before he was to leave. He had managed to get the use of his father's car, and they drove out of the city along the river and parked in a narrow road. There at last, at the last moment before the long summer, they crossed the boundary at which they had always stopped before. In the experience for her there was some sadness and a little pain and, most of all, an oddly exciting sense of charity, as if she had, at some sacrifice, been kind to a child who needed her.

He went away the next day to the university, and a little later he wrote to her, and she replied. He wrote again, telling her that he was already looking forward to Christmas, when he would come home and see her, and she replied again and told him that she was also looking forward to it. Then in

November she got a letter saying that his parents had moved away from St. Louis to a small town across state and that he wouldn't be able to see her at Christmas after all. At first, for a while, after the intimacy by the river and his going away, she had felt desolate and alone in a drained and distorted world, and she had thought then that she truly loved him and would die without him. But in time the color returned surely to the world around her, her perspective returned, and she was able to admit to herself what she had known all along, that he was an oversensitive and unstable boy who would never on earth do one thing of consequence. When the last letter came, she did not answer it.

CHAPTER III

Late that Sunday afternoon the snow stopped falling, and Donna returned from the narrow, oppressive house to her apartment. It was dark when she got there, and she stood a few moments in the unlighted living room, wondering how she could survive the long night. She could not remember ever having been so tired before, and she felt in her stomach a dull and gnawing pain that reminded her that she had not eaten since the dinner the night before that she and Aaron had eaten together in celebration of the sale of the peau de soie. The dinner seemed a long time ago and scarcely credible as something that had actually happened. By a kind of strange reversal of chronology in her mind, perhaps because the present was a threat she needed for a while to evade, recent events were indistinct, and the clearest were those which were furthest away.

Crossing the dark living room, she went into the bedroom and turned on a light and undressed. After a hot shower, her second of the day, she put on pajamas and went into the kitchen. She did not want to eat, for even the thought of food was slightly sickening to her, but she knew from the gnawing pain in her stomach that she had better eat something. She heated a can of soup on the range, and sat down at the small breakfast table in a corner of the room to eat it with crackers. After she finished the soup she felt a little sustained, and the night ahead of her seemed a little less impossible.

She washed the pan and bowl and spoon she had used and returned to the living room. At a cabinet, she mixed a very strong drink, half bourbon and half seltzer, and then setting the drink on a small table beside a large brocaded chair, she went to a console phonograph, selected an album of Chopin waltzes, and put the recordings on the spindle. The first platter dropped softly to the spinning, felt-covered turntable, and the ineffably precise and delicate music came alive in the room. She sat down and drank from her glass and began to go over in her mind how she could arrange the finding of Aaron in the morning.

For it would be necessary, of course, to wait until morning. At least, if not necessary, it would be wise. It could be done naturally then, a normal gesture when he did not appear at the shop. Perhaps she could send someone from the shop, or go herself and discover him by looking into the hall through the glass of the front door, or call a neighbor or a friend or even the police to investigate his inexplicable absence. Yes, any one of these actions would seem natural, an expression of concern in which she would be supported by Gussie Ingram and everyone else at the shop, and no particular attention or suspicion could possibly attach to her because of it. It could make no difference to him if he lay untended in the hall for another night. It was only in her mind that it made a difference, and it was imperative that she stop thinking as if he were somehow alive and dead at the same time, somehow aware of his desertion and the loneliness and the cold.

And then, all at once, she thought of the cleaning woman, and she could not understand how she had failed to think of her immediately, long ago at the very beginning, when she had found the body. That she had failed to do so was certainly an indication of the extent she had been incapacitated by shock without fully realizing it. Aaron himself had spoken of the cleaning woman more than once—a Mrs. Cassidy, or a similar Irish name—and had said she had a key and came in to clean two days a week, two of them. (It was always planned that Donna should not be there the mornings she came.) Thinking back and trying to identify the days, Donna was certain that they were Monday and Friday. Tomorrow was Monday. Therefore Mrs. Cassidy, or whatever her name was, would surely come in the morning and find the body, and it would be unnecessary, after all, for Donna to take any action whatever.

This was a vast relief. It was so vast a relief, and left her so limp in the sudden release from pressure, that she became fully aware then, for the first time, how much she had been dreading the prospect of taking any action. Now she need only wait with patience and react appropriately to whatever developed.

Getting out of the chair, she turned the stack of recordings over on the spindle and set the mechanism again and went into the bedroom. In bed, she lay and listened to the waltzes, trying to remember as little as possible and to anticipate nothing at all. She knew very little about music and had little knowledge about the Chopin she was listening to, but she did know that the music made everything else seem *less* important for the time that she listened to it. With their help, and that of the strong drink, she went into a dreamless sleep and awakened early the next morning.

After dressing, she had coffee in the kitchen and went directly to the shop, arriving about an hour before the shop normally opened. She entered by the front door, locking it after her, and passed through the luxurious simplicity of the salon to her room at the rear. There, she began without delay to work on a half-completed sketch, and she worked, apparently with complete absorption, until she heard, after half an hour, Gussie Ingram at the rear door. She went out then and let Gussie in and returned to the room with Gussie following.

"Snow!" Gussie said bitterly. "God, how I hate the filthy stuff! To think that there are places in the world, on this very continent, where the sun is warm and the days are long and there isn't one snotty nose or congested chest or any of this Goddamn virus stuff that the doctor always says you've got when he doesn't know. Honest to God, a person must be insane to live in a hellish place like this."

"Why do you live in it, then?"

"Because I'm insane, darling. Hadn't you guessed? We're all insane. If we weren't, we'd simply swallow a bellyful of sleeping pills, or use any one of the many other pleasant and painless methods of getting out of this filthy mess for good and all instead of hanging on and on for more of the same."

Filthy was one of her favorite words. She slumped into a chair and began to cough, covering her mouth with a pink tissue. After a while she stopped coughing and lit a cigarette and immediately began to cough again. Watching her, Donna thought that she looked tired and ill, even more tired and more ill than she usually looked. She was, in fact, quite an ugly woman, but it was a striking kind of ugliness that had its own kind of appeal. Her skin was sallow, stretched tightly over the frame of her face and emphasizing the size of a nose and mouth that were large yet lacked emphasis. The cords in her neck became prominent when she turned her head, and her body was thin to the point of emaciation, collar and hip bones threatening, it seemed, to tear through their thin coating of flesh. There was grace in her gauntness, though, an unorthodox smartness in the way she walked and gestured and wore her clothes. Donna often wondered how old she was, and was sure that she was neither young nor old nor any particular age at all, a woman arrested and fixed who would go on and on all her life without ever looking a day older, just closer to dying.

"That's a nasty cough," Donna said. "Wouldn't you like to go home and take care of it?"

"No, thanks." Gussie extended her legs and blew smoke at her feet. "Another day alone at home with my sweet thoughts is the last thing I want. I'll gobble lozenges till quitting time and whisky till bedtime, and I'll manage to survive for a while yet."

"Did you have a bad Sunday?" Donna asked.

"Filthy. Utterly filthy. I thought the damn day would never end. Not you, I'll bet. You must have gone on a real fancy kick."

"Why?"

"Because of the peau de soie, I mean. It isn't every day you can hang four hundred dollars' worth of your own talent on someone like Queen Hattie Tyler. Not that the one sale in itself is so much. It's what it means to your future, darling."

"Well, I didn't really go on a very fancy kick. Aaron took me out to dinner and then out to Mother's. I spent the night and practically all of yesterday there. Do you actually think the sale to Harriet Tyler will turn into something?"

Gussie dragged on her cigarette and coughed the smoke out of her lungs. Her wide, ugly mouth stretched into a smile as she looked at Donna through the blue thinning cloud.

"I'll be damned surprised if it doesn't. You know why? Because you've got it, darling. You've got the feel or the touch or whatever the hell you want to call it. That little thing that the rest of us haven't got and would give our souls to have. The job you sold Hattie was a perfect conception and a flawless execution, and you can't say any more than that for any gown. It'll stand out in any crowd with any comparison, and Hattie will look just like her precious William Walter's millions because she's got something to give to the gown as well as to get from it. I hate the bitch, but I'll have to admit she's stacked properly, and every slob and scarecrow who sees her in the gown will get the idea they'd look the same in one like it. Oh, don't worry, darling, they'll follow Hattie, and Hattie will be back. You've got what it takes to get what you want, and now it'll begin coming with Hattie and the rest, and I'm damn glad of it, because I like you. That makes you exclusive, darling, whether you know it or not, for the people I like are very few. I could count the people I like on the fingers of one hand."

"Thanks, Gussie. I like you, too. Better than anyone else, I think. You know that."

"Sure, I know it. There's a kind of rare and holy bond between us that's just too precious for words, so let's forget it. For God's sake, I couldn't stand any sloppy scenes this morning. You say you spent Saturday night and Sunday at your mother's?"

"That's right. Aaron drove me out after dinner."

"I commend your devotion, darling. To me, it seems a filthy dull way to waste a night that should have been celebrated."

"Aaron wasn't feeling well, as a matter of fact. I think he wanted to get to bed early."

"His heart again?"

"I don't know. He didn't say it was that."

"He never does. Just totes his little detonating pills around, in case. Probably one of these days he'll pop off in an instant, and it's a filthy shame because he's a sweet guy. He's a sweet, lonely, damned little apostate, and he's another one of the fingers on the hand I count my friends on."

The words invoked in Donna's mind the image of Aaron as the words were spoken, Aaron alone and dead and damned, and she closed her eyes upon the image, trapping it behind her lids. Then, in succession, came the sound of the rear door opening and closing, the brisk swishing of galoshes outside, and the near, softer sound of Gussie's long sighing.

"That'll be Serena," Gussie said. "God bless her pretty little pointed head."

Serena was a saleslady and sometime model, Gussie's subordinate. She was a pale blonde with a tall willowy body and almost perfect classical features that were, fortunately, only slightly blemished by vacuity.

"Oh, come off it, Gussie," Donna said. "You know very well you consider Serena a valuable employee."

"Of course I do," Gussie admitted, "but I am constantly amazed by the girl's absolutely perfect stupidity. In its way, it's every bit as perfect as her face."

"That's all right. A girl with Serena's looks doesn't have to have brains."

"No, darling, you're wrong there." Gussie shook her head and leaned forward to crush her cigarette in a tray. "A girl with Serena's looks needs brains more than most of us. In just her face and body, without anything in addition, she has the most useful tools that a woman can have on earth, but she has to have the brains to use them effectively. It staggers the imagination to consider what things she might accomplish for herself if she were only a little clever, and it's horribly depressing to know what a monstrous waste Serena is bound to make of them. Do you know that she's in love? It's the truth, so help me God, and it's simply the filthiest kind of a shame. She's in love with a kid who's a bookkeeper in a department store and will be a bookkeeper in a department store forever, and they're only waiting until he gets a lousy ten-dollar raise or something so they can be married. She is simply too stupid to understand that she could just as easily go to bed with the goddamn owner if only she knew how to use what she's got." Gussie stood up abruptly and moved toward the door. "Oh, well, the hell with it! It's no skin off my tail. I'd better go get things open up front. If Queen Hattie wore that gown during the weekend, we may have an early rush for Donna Buchanan originals."

Donna laughed, though she didn't feel at all like laughing. The increasing pressure about Aaron and what could possibly be developing in connection with him was bad enough, and now Gussie's chatter about Serena's waste of her assets had made matters even worse and more depressing by reminding her of her mother, who had also wasted what she might have used.

Gussie gone, she resumed work on her sketch, but she was unable to accomplish anything that pleased her. Her feeling of guilt was developing abnormally to include much more than her legitimate responsibility, not only her evasion of a clear obligation, if not actually a betrayal of trust, but also an irrational feeling of having been instrumental, somehow, in Aaron's death. It would have been a relief to confide in Gussie, to call her back and tell her just what had happened and to achieve in the telling a measure of catharsis. She was not restrained by a lack of confidence in Gussie, for she knew very well that Gussie would collaborate in good faith. She truly did not know what restrained her, but only that she had better adhere to the policy of solitary deception, except for her mother, that she had set for herself.

After she had worked with little effect for about an hour, she got up and went forward into the salon; it was then a few minutes after ten o'clock. Both Gussie and Serena were busy with customers, and she waited at the rear, smoking a cigarette, until Gussie was free and came back to her.

"Has Aaron come in?" she said.

"Not yet." Gussie removed a thin brown lozenge from a box and put it on her tongue. "I'm satisfied these filthy things will destroy me in a little while, but in the meantime they keep me from coughing. Perhaps he's still not feeling well and won't come in at all."

"I don't know. There is something I particularly want to speak with him about, and he assured me Saturday night that he would be here this morning."

"It's only around ten, darling. Probably he'll be here soon."

"His wife's not at home, you know."

"Yes, I know. That hypochondriac bitch is gone off to Florida again, and don't I hate her guts because she's there instead of me." Gussie stared at Donna intently. "But why mention his wife? What's the significance?"

"Nothing, I guess. I was just thinking that he's all alone in the house. Do you suppose anything could have happened to him?"

"Like another heart attack?"

"Yes."

Gussie's face expressed a kind of undirected anger at the filthiness of things in general.

"Damn it, darling, let's not start anticipating anything. If he's not here in another hour, we can call his house or something."

Donna returned to her room and sat down to the sketch, but she no longer tried to work. The promotion of deception, especially her easy accomplishment of it, filled her with self-disgust and actually made her physically ill. After a few minutes, she got up and went out and opened the door to Aaron's office so that she could hear the phone in there if it began to ring. Then she returned and sat down again and stared at the sketch without seeing it, and waited and waited for the ringing to begin. Surely Mrs. Cassidy—was that her name?—had arrived long ago at the house to discover Aaron in the hall, and if she had discovered him, which she surely had, what had she done about it? What would one do naturally in such an event? It was quite likely that she had first called a doctor, even though Aaron was obviously dead and had been dead for a long time and had no need of a doctor, simply because calling a doctor was what one would instinctively think of and do. The doctor would come and would in turn call the police. The police would come, and all this would take time, of course, but surely there had been time enough. Surely they were there now, or had been there, and why in God's name didn't one of them call the shop, which would seem a reasonable thing to do.

Sitting and waiting and visualizing the probable sequence of events, she felt her tension increasing to an intolerable degree. She wanted desperately to get up and do something to relieve it—to run or scream or destroy something with her hands, or best of all to call Aaron's home number at once and get it over with—but she knew that it would not be wise to display an anxiety out of proportion to its cause. So she forced herself to sit and wait with apparent calm until most of another hour had passed. At ten minutes to eleven, Gussie came into the room, and it was she who assumed in the end the position of suggesting some kind of action.

"Damn it, Donna," she said, "you've started me worrying. I think I'll call Aaron's house. Not that it'll do any good, so far as I can see. If he's there alone, and something's happened to him, he won't be able to answer."

"A cleaning woman comes in some days. She might be there this morning."

"That's right. I'd forgotten about her. Do you think I should call?"

"No." Donna stood up. "I'll call, Gussie. I was just thinking about doing it when you came in."

She went out of the room and into Aaron's office. Gussie followed and stood in the doorway, watching her as she dialed the number. At the other end of the line, the telephone rang in three long bursts, and at the completion of the third burst the receiver was picked up and a man's voice came through.

"Hello," the voice said.

"Hello." There was a painful constriction in Donna's throat, and she could not understand how her own voice slipped so easily through it. "Is this Aaron Burns' residence?"

"Yes."

"Is Mr. Burns there?"

"He's here, but he can't come to the phone. Who's calling, please?"

"This is Donna Buchanan, Mr. Burns' assistant."

"Assistant?"

"At the shop."

"Would you care to tell me what you want with Mr. Burns?"

"I don't think so. At least, not unless you would first care to tell me who you are."

"Sorry. My name's Daniels. I'm a policeman."

"Policeman! What's the matter? Has something happened to Mr. Burns?"

"I'm afraid so. As a matter of fact, he's dead."

"Dead? Mr. Burns is dead?"

"Right, Miss Buchanan. He's dead."

"Why are the police there?"

"He was alone when he died, Miss Buchanan. The cleaning woman found him when she arrived for work this morning. It's required that the police make a routine investigation of such matters."

"I see. Was it his heart?"

"I wouldn't know, Miss Buchanan. I'm a policeman, not a doctor. What makes you think it might have been his heart?"

"Because he's had heart attacks before. The cleaning woman should be able to tell you that."

"She has done so, as a matter of fact. To be perfectly frank with you, Mr. Burns' doctor said it was his heart, and it probably was, but it isn't official yet."

"Thank you for being frank."

"Have I offended you? If I have, I'm sorry. I realize that this must be quite a shock to you."

"Thank you for being sorry."

"Well, I don't seem to be doing very well with you, Miss Buchanan. Perhaps I'd have better luck if I spoke with you in person. Would you agree to see me for a few minutes?"

"You mean you want me to come out to the house?"

"That won't be necessary. I'd be happy to call at the shop."

"All right."

"Thank you, Miss Buchanan. Some time this afternoon. Probably about two o'clock."

Now that it was over, she felt drained and spent and suddenly chilled, and she put her head in her hands and began to shiver. Gussie moved over quickly from the door to put an arm around her shoulders, and the scent of Gussie was an odd and offensive mixture of perfume and smoke and medicated lozenges.

"So he's dead," Gussie said quietly. "We all knew it would happen sooner or later, darling. For God's sake, don't fall apart on me."

"I'm all right," Donna said. "I'm perfectly all right."

2

It was two-thirty when Daniels came. She was aware at once that he was not at all what she would have imagined if she had imagined anything. He was slender, almost slight, dressed neatly in a gray suit with which he wore a white shirt and maroon knit tie and black shoes, and in the rich simplicity of the shop he seemed neither out of place nor ill at ease. He sat down with motion that seemed almost practiced, a suggestion of exceptional coordination and of strength in excess of its first impression. His hair was light brown, cut close to his head, and his eyes were brown and as light as his hair, having at times a yellowish cast.

"I'm afraid I upset you on the telephone this morning, Miss Buchanan," he said. "I'm sorry."

"Not at all," she said.

"Nevertheless, it must have been a shock to learn of Mr. Burns' death in such a manner."

"It was a shock, but it was not entirely unexpected. We all knew that he had a heart condition."

"That's been established. Two previous attacks, I believe."

"I think so. He had one since I became associated with him."

"I see. Well, it's now certain that he died of another attack. Early Sunday morning, as nearly as it can be fixed. It's probable that he simply dropped over without ever knowing what happened to him."

"If it was necessary for him to die, I'm glad that it was that way."

"Yes, I suppose it's easier if it happens quickly. Sometimes I wonder, though, if I wouldn't like to have a little time to die in. A little time at the end, I mean, to try to put things together and make some kind of sense of them." The thin light of his smile flared briefly and went out. "Just an odd notion, of course."

She thought herself that it was odd, especially coming from him, from whom she would not have expected it. It suggested that he had thought seriously about the matter and had developed already, though he was still young, a kind of prospectus for dying. Looking at him with an interest that was more than what he had originally evoked because of his role in her own situation, she wondered what kind of man he was—what books he read, what music he listened to, how and to whom he might make love.

When she made no response to his thoughts on dying, he said, "Did you know Mr. Burns well, Miss Buchanan?"

"Quite well, I think. I worked with him closely and enjoyed his confidence, if that's what you mean."

"You referred to yourself as his assistant. What does that mean, precisely?"

"I don't know that it means anything very precise. I design gowns which are sold in this shop, and I managed the business when he was recovering from his second heart attack."

"That's certainly indicative of confidence, I'd say. Did you know him socially as well?"

"We occasionally had dinner together."

"Nothing more than that?"

"I'm not quite sure what you are trying to get at. Are you making an implication I should resent?"

"I hope not. I'd only like to know if he ever spoke to you about his personal life."

"It's very likely, isn't it? It would hardly have been natural if he hadn't. Only a minute or two ago you were telling me yourself, though I've just met you, your personal feelings about dying."

"So I was." He paused and stared down at his feet for a moment. "Let me put it this way. Did Mr. Burns give the impression of being a happy man?"

"Happy? I don't think I could say. I don't even think I know what happiness is."

"I'm very certain that I don't, so far as that goes, but you're equivocating, Miss Buchanan. Taking happiness to be merely a reasonably good adjustment to life, would you be willing to say that he was happy?"

"He was successful and adjusted and, if you insist on your term, I suppose he was happy."

"From Mr. Burns' housekeeper this morning, I gathered that his marriage was not successful. Is that so?"

"Are you prepared to credit the gossip of a cleaning woman about something like that?"

"Not at all. That's why I'm asking for your opinion."

"All right. His marriage was not successful, but it did not disturb him. He had reached a point where it no longer meant anything to him, one way or another. If you are thinking that he might have committed suicide because of it, you are certainly mistaken."

"I don't think he committed suicide. When I told you it was established that he died of a heart attack, I was telling you the truth."

"In that case, why are you still concerned as a policeman? Why am I compelled to answer your questions?"

"You are not compelled to answer. You are not compelled to talk to me at all. Frankly, there is something in this that disturbs me, and I hope you will answer a few more questions voluntarily in order to help me clarify it for myself."

"What is it that disturbs you?"

"Are you willing, then, to help?"

"I can't think what could possibly concern you in Aaron's death, since it's established as natural, but I'll help you if I can."

"Thank you. Many men, when their marriages turn out badly, look for satisfaction elsewhere. With other women, or another woman. Did Mr. Burns do that?"

"I don't think I'll answer that question."

"Your refusal to answer indicates that he did."

"Nothing of the sort. It indicates that you are certainly prying into something that is none of your business."

"Look, Miss Buchanan. I'm no moralist. At least I am not functioning as a moralist in this instance. Perhaps I had better tell you what I have in mind."

"Perhaps you had."

"All right. I strongly suspect that a woman spent the night, or part of it, with Mr. Burns. The night before his death. She may have left, of course, before his death, or she may not have, and I would like to know which way it was."

"If she was there at all."

"Of course. If she was there at all."

"Why do you think she may have been?"

"It's usually pretty apparent when two people have slept in a bed."

"No cigarettes with lipstick on them?"

"No, nothing so obvious." He smiled thinly. "Are you being sarcastic, Miss Buchanan?"

"I'm sorry."

"It's all right. I am probably being a bore, so I don't really blame you. As a matter of fact, however, the absence of lipstick-stained stubs is a point in itself. A kind of negative one. If other signs indicate a woman's presence, the missing stubs would seem to suggest that she may have left after his death, since she took the trouble to dispose of them. Sudden death during an assignation, even natural death, would make a nasty mess that any woman would prefer to avoid."

"Perhaps she didn't smoke. Perhaps she simply didn't want the housekeeper to know she'd been there. Perhaps Aaron disposed of them after she was gone. If she was ever there."

"You needn't restate the condition every time, Miss Buchanan. It's thoroughly understood. All the points you make are possible, of course, and you are clever to think of them so quickly. It took me a while longer. Now all I have is a bed which appears to have been slept in by two people." He took a package of cigarettes from his pocket and, leaning forward, extended it toward her. "Do you smoke?"

"Yes, thank you."

She took a cigarette and accepted his light and drew smoke deeply into her lungs. He thought, watching her, that she was a very attractive and clever young woman, to say nothing of being an extremely self-possessed one. She was, in fact, the very kind of young woman that he himself would like to have. When she held out the cigarette so that he could see clearly the vivid stain on the end that had been between her lips, he looked at it and up at her and smiled again his thin smile.

"I have nothing to compare it with, Miss Buchanan. Besides, even if I did, it would prove nothing definitely."

"Do you really wish to prove something definitely? Couldn't you prove it by fingerprints or something like that?"

"I might prove that someone had been there. I couldn't prove when. Anyhow, there was definitely nothing extraordinary in Mr. Burns' death, and I am not particularly anxious to flay a straw man."

"Why are you doing it, then?"

"Am I? Perhaps I am. It's only that I always feel a strong compulsion to gather up a loose end."

"How do you intend to gather it?"

"When I came here, I had a couple of devious tactics in mind. Now that I have met you and talked with you, I prefer to ask directly if you were with Mr. Burns when he died, or in the house the night before."

"I'll not answer that, of course. Your loose end, I think, must remain ungathered."

"Do you think so? As for me, I think I'll just consider it safely tucked in." He stood up and extended a hand which, after a moment, she accepted. "It's been a pleasure, Miss Buchanan. You're a most attractive woman."

"Thank you."

"I'd enjoy very much seeing you again, but I suppose that's impossible."

"I suppose it is."

"Goodby, then."

"Goodby."

In the evening after the shop closed Gussie stopped in before going home. "How did it go with the copper?" she asked. "He was only trying to gather up a loose end."

"What kind of loose end?"

"He thinks someone may have spent Saturday night with Aaron."

"A woman?"

"Yes. Of course."

"Does he think she may have had something to do with his death?"

"Oh, no. Nothing like that. It's definite that he died naturally of a heart attack."

"Then why the hell does he care who may have slept there? I don't get it."

"Well, I suppose it's some kind of offense of omission if you know about a death and don't report it. He didn't seem inclined to make much of an issue of it, however."

Gussie leaned her head back against the chair and closed her eyes.

"Was a woman there with Aaron, darling?"

"How would I know?"

"You'd know if you were the woman, wouldn't you?"

"Do you think I was having an affair with Aaron?"

"Affair? That's a fancy word that I wouldn't know about. I know damn well you were sleeping with him."

"What makes you so sure?"

"Darling, darling, this is old Gussie speaking. You don't have to play cat and mouse with me. I've slept with enough men myself to be able to tell when one's being slept with. Especially one like Aaron, who simply exuded gratitude and devotion. Don't you think I've seen him looking at you?"

"I didn't dream that it was so apparent."

"To no one but Gussie, darling."

"Do you blame me, Gussie?"

"God, no! Don't be absurd, darling." Gussie laughed softly. "He was a starved and lonely guy with a thousand vague oppressions, married to a bitch and living from habit. He needed you and had you, and I'm glad. I truly loved the sad bastard in my own way, and I'd have slept with him myself if he'd ever asked me."

Watching Gussie's face, like a death mask with its closed eyes, Donna had for the first time an intimation of just what burden of grief might now be carried in Gussie's heart, silently in the bony body. It had not once occurred to her that Gussie might feel for Aaron any emotion beyond the ordinary. And she was ashamed that Gussie had been so sentient, while she had been so dull. She was also ashamed she had lied to Gussie about Saturday night. She would have liked now to renounce the lie, but she couldn't quite bring herself to do it. So she decided, as a compromise, to tell still another lie that would at least embrace part of the truth.

"The truth is," she said, "I went to Aaron's, but I didn't stay all night. We went there after dinner, and later he took me out to Mother's."

"Did you tell the copper that?"

"No. I didn't think it was necessary. I refused to answer his questions about it."

"Well, under the circumstances, that's merely a way of telling him everything without committing yourself to anything. I shouldn't worry about it if I were you, darling, and if you need any expert lying done, don't fail to call on Gussie. I've had a lot of experience, and I'm one of the most convincing liars on earth."

"Thanks, Gussie."

Donna stood up and walked around the room, stretching the muscles of her back and legs. She felt exhausted by the tensions of the day, and she was thankful it was over. Her head throbbed, and she pressed her hand against her forehead.

"Is everyone gone?" she said.

"Yes. I assumed the authority to tell them not to come in tomorrow. Was I right?"

"Of course. We must certainly remain closed at least until after Aaron is buried."

"What will be done about the shop, I wonder."

"I don't know. It will be up to Aaron's wife, I suppose. His widow. It's a fine shop, and it's getting better all the time, and if she's wise she will let it continue to make money for her."

"She's not wise. She's a stupid, lazy slut who likes to lie on her tail and play sick, and it's my opinion that she'll convert her responsibilities into cash as quickly as possible."

"I hope not."

"So do I, but I shouldn't count on it. It will be a damn, shame if she does, especially for you, darling, now that you've got started so beautifully with your originals."

"I've been thinking about it—about the shop, I mean, and what will happen to it—and perhaps I'll go and talk to Mrs. Burns about it."

"To try to sell her on keeping it open?"

"Yes. I could manage it for her, Gussie. With your help I know I could do it. I did it while Aaron was in the hospital the last time, and I could do it permanently if she would only let me."

"Of course you could, darling. Your judgment is as good as Aaron's was, and you have other assets that he lacked. Actually, given a free hand, you would certainly make a bigger thing of the shop than he could have."

"Do you think she will let me, Gussie?"

"I told you that I don't, and I don't. I'm sorry, darling, but she simply won't want to be bothered with it."

"What shall we do if she refuses?"

"Look for jobs, I guess. What the hell else will there be to do?"

Donna stood quietly for a moment, gnawing a knuckle.

"Damn her to hell," she said. "She tried her best to ruin Aaron's life, and now, because she is a stupid woman, she'll ruin ours if we don't stop her. Gussie, how much do you think the shop would sell for?"

"I don't know. As a guess, two hundred thousand. Certainly no less. Why?"

"I was wondering if it would be possible to buy it. For me to buy it."

"I don't know where you'd get two hundred thousand dollars, or even two hundred thousand cents in a hurry, but I know where we can get a good strong drink, which is available and at the moment even more essential. Are you interested?"

"No." Donna shook her head. "Thanks just the same, Gussie, but I think I'll stay on for a while."

"All right, darling. If you want me, you know where to find me. Take care, now."

Gussie went out, and Donna sat down and removed her glasses and began to rub her eyes. She heard the rear door open and close as Gussie left and continued to sit and rub her eyes, wondering how she could best approach Aaron's widow, or how she could possibly get hold of enormous amounts of money like two hundred thousand dollars.

CHAPTER IV

Sharkey Mulloy was a man who loved his work. Those who saw Sharkey on the streets of St. Louis were never aware that in him existed a glimmer of the glory that had been Greece, a speck of the grandeur that had been Rome. It was true that there were some, even in this enlightened age, who considered his work pagan in practice and sinful in nature, but even Sir Thomas Browne, himself a Christian, was unable to discredit entirely this vestige of Christian idiocy.

Now, this day, Sharkey sat in a vault below a chapel and listened to the sound of a mourning organ. He could hear the organ only faintly, and he wished he could not hear it at all, for he did not like it. He did not, as a matter of fact, like anything about what was now going on in the chapel, for he considered it a sticky business better eliminated. A realist, however, he accepted it as a necessary prelude to his own work, something to be tolerated out of deference to deluded folk who paid the tariff but couldn't understand the proper way of doing a thing. After the organ was silent and the chapel was empty, when what was left came down on the elevator into his hands, things would be different and better by far. The whole complex and obscure confusion of dogma and display would become, under his definitive ministration, serene and clear, and pure as fire.

In due time he heard the elevator descending and went out to receive his charge from Mr. Fairstead, who always made the delivery himself in what Sharkey had to admit was a nice gesture in the last phase of a last rite. Today, as usual, Mr. Fairstead looked somber below the neck and quite cheerful above, and his voice, when he spoke, agreed with the part above.

"Well, here he is, Sharkey," he said. "Be sure to give us back our three percent."

"Net," Sharkey said.

Mr. Fairstead laughed and went, the elevator groaning upward, and Sharkey took over, warmed as always by the intimate little exchange that had not varied a bit in twenty years, except that the personal pronoun changed its gender to suit the occasion. He worked swiftly and efficiently, and it required only a short while to complete in the vault what had been begun in the chapel, to make in action the grand consignment that had already been made in words. This done, and with a period of waiting now to be endured, Sharkey put on his hat and went around the corner to a tavern.

He returned to his vault after an hour and read an Agatha Christie murder mystery for something over another hour. Finally, the time past, he extracted Mr. Fairstead's three percent, and extracted with a magnet from the three percent a number of long screws. All screws removed, he put the three percent in a temporary receptacle and sealed it. On the outside of the receptacle, he stuck a gummed label on which he had previously printed in clear block letters: **BURNS, AARON—SPLENDID IN ASHES.**

He was actually required to print only the name. The added little epitaph, a phrase lifted from Browne's *Hydriotaphia,* was Sharkey's own idea.

2

The residue of Aaron Burns, the three percent that Mr. Fairstead facetiously claimed and Sharkey Mulloy carefully preserved, really belonged, of course, to Shirley Smith Burns, his widow, who did not linger to claim her property. Arrangements with Mr. Fairstead for a suitable urn and a perpetual-care niche in the chapel of the crematorium had been completed, and there seemed nothing left for her to do. Besides, she was feeling quite ghastly, and she had this odd sensation of her skull's being packed loosely with sawdust which shifted about in the most peculiar manner every time she moved her head. She was being driven home by Earl Joslin, Aaron's lawyer, and she thought with resignation, looking out the car window at the remnants of snow, that it was unfortunate that she had been compelled to hurry all the way back from Florida at such an inconvenient time.

Many things in the life of Shirley Smith Burns had been, and were still, unfortunate. Perhaps the single most unfortunate thing—though it is actually impossible ever to pinpoint this—was the diphtheria which she had as a child. This was the only genuinely organic illness she ever had in her life, and she very nearly died of it, but all in all, in the final stages of recovery, she enjoyed it immensely. She was extravagantly loved and coddled and waited upon. She was the significant center of her universe. The romance of the experience, as well as the attention, was not lost upon her, for there is something poetic in the mortality of a child, and no one is more aware of it than children.

For a long time she amused herself by playing imaginative variations on the theme of her death, and it was too bad, in a way, that she could not actually have died. The only reservations she felt in this childish death wish were the knowledge that she would be unable to attend the funeral. She recovered from the diphtheria, but she never recovered from the convalescence. Moreover and worse, neither did her mother. She, having seen her only child imperiled, waged thereafter a continuing terrified battle against all the shadows of death. And Shirley grew up in the shadows. Later, when she was grown, when impatience and indifference succeeded concern, it was too late to come out from these shadows.

This change did not occur until she lost her mother. That intrepid woman, constantly alert to the designs of Death upon her daughter, was careless of his designs upon herself, and she let him steal up on her. She died suddenly one spring, and the following winter her husband died of a bronchial pneumonia he might have survived if he had not learned from his family to despise and avoid doctors.

Shirley was left with a modest income from investments and an endless repertoire of psychosomatic ills, and eventually, by chance or fate or the caprice of the devil, she met and married Aaron Burns. She married him for several reasons, and none of them was love. Most compelling of the reasons was that he was gentle enough to be imposed upon and clever enough to make lots of money. But what she was never capable of learning was that he needed most of all, because of his spiritual desolation, a simple carnal acceptance in the broad meaning of the terms. Unable to give him this in even a narrow sense, let alone a broad one, she left it to someone else.

She was a selfish woman, but she was no fool. She was certainly aware, after she began denying him herself, that he was getting satisfaction elsewhere. She never suspected, however, his actual method before Donna, and it would have been better for her if she had. She thought that he probably kept a mistress, despising him for it as a man too weak for pure devotion, but she never despised herself for her part in it. The irrational thing about her reaction was the really virulent hatred she developed for the woman who was giving and getting what she herself did not care to give or accept, and there was a time when she felt that it was absolutely necessary, if she was to retain her sanity, to know who the woman was. She hired a detective to follow Aaron for one month, but the detective, a reasonable fellow who did not consider a whorehouse and a mistress synonymous, submitted a negative report. After that she did not try to discover the identity of the woman, but she remained convinced that she existed, certain in her own mind that the detective was an incompetent and Aaron a monster of deception. She found solace in suffering, and began going frequently to Florida.

They turned into the drive and stopped beside the house, and Joslin came around to open the door on her side of the car. With one hand lightly on her elbow, he assisted her into the house and upstairs, and waited in the hall outside her room until she called to him to enter. When he went in, she was reclining on a chaise longue, wearing a pale negligee that emphasized the pallor of her skin and the shadows under her eyes. She incited in him a kind of delicate crawling revulsion, a faint unpleasant tickling below the diaphragm. He was here because he was Aaron's lawyer and because of a genuine liking and regret for Aaron himself. But as soon as he had settled Aaron's affairs, he never again wanted to see Aaron's widow.

"You look exhausted," he said courteously. "Don't you think we had better postpone everything for a few days?"

"No. I'm feeling better now, and I want your advice about several things. Tell me again the terms of the will."

"They're quite simple. Everything comes to you except the two bequests to Miss Ingram and Miss Buchanan."

"One thousand to Miss Ingram and ten to Miss Buchanan?"

"That's right."

"It's quite a substantial difference. I wonder why."

"As I told you, Miss Buchanan is quite a talented young woman. Her original designs have contributed a great deal to the reputation of the shop, and you may remember that she managed the business very competently when Aaron was laid up with his second heart attack. I'm sure the ten thousand is only a kind of bonus in recognition of these services."

"Which one was she?"

"At the chapel?"

"Yes, of course."

"The one with glasses. Quite a striking young woman, I think."

He paid the compliment in malice, but he paid it deftly with the intent and without the appearance. "Can the will be broken?" she asked. "Just the two bequests, you mean?"

"Naturally."

"No. I can see no possibility at all. Even if there were, I'd hardly advise it. After all, the amount involved is insignificant compared to the total estate. The action would cost too much for so little. Moreover, if you'll excuse my saying so, I feel that Aaron's last wishes should be respected."

"It's the principle. You know perfectly well what everyone will think when this woman receives such a large amount."

"Oh, nonsense. I'm sure no one will think anything of the sort. Besides, a court action would certainly be a poor way of detracting attention."

"All right, I won't make an issue of it if you think I shouldn't. I want your opinion on the shop."

"What about the shop?"

"What would you estimate it is worth?"

"Off hand, it's impossible to be accurate. I'd guess not less than two hundred thousand dollars as it now stands."

"Will it be difficult to find a buyer?"

"I shouldn't think so. Its reputation is superb. Probably has the most desirable patronage in town. However, if you really want my opinion, I advise you not to sell."

"Why not?"

"The shop is a highly successful enterprise. Nowhere else could you invest your money to receive such large returns."

"I'm not a business woman. Besides, I am not well. I couldn't possibly run it."

"Of course not. You would have to employ a manager who is skilled in that type of business."

"I wouldn't even be able to judge the efficiency of a manager. I'd be vulnerable to all sorts of errors and impositions."

"Do you still want my advice?"

"Certainly. That's why I asked you to stay."

"Very well, then. I advise you to keep the shop and to keep Miss Buchanan as its manager."

"The woman who gets the bequest?"

"That's right. Donna Buchanan. I know that Aaron had the highest regard for her, and I know from other sources that she's truly a fine designer. The line of originals she's initiated compares favorably, I'm told, with the best anywhere, and it's gaining recognition from women who are willing and able to pay very fancy prices for their original gowns. There's simply no way to estimate the potential of this kind of enterprise."

"No. I don't wish to be encumbered with it. I wish to liquidate all assets and leave this city as soon as possible."

"Just as you say, of course."

"Will you handle it for me?"

"Certainly."

"That's settled, then."

"You understand, I hope, that the final settlement of an estate requires time."

"Oh, yes. Naturally. Just expedite it as much as you can." She closed her eyes, pressing her fingers upon the lids. "Now I think I had better rest. It has been a difficult day, and I'm really feeling quite ill. Please excuse me for not seeing you out."

"It's perfectly all right."

He stood up. Screened by her lowered lids, he permitted his revulsion to show for a moment in his face. Turning, he walked silently out of the room and downstairs and out of the house.

Behind him, on the lounge in the room where Donna had lately walked with pride in herself and contempt for the room's owner, Shirley Burns lay quietly with her eyes still closed. She had told for once the truth about herself. She was really quite ill with a functional illness, and the illness was fury and hate.

Her lips moved soundlessly in the shape of an epithet.

3

From the crematorium chapel, Donna and Gussie walked together to a stop where they caught, after a few minutes, a bus downtown. They got off near the shop and walked from there to a nearby cocktail lounge. Entering it, they sat at a tiny table in a corner. Soft light was admitted through perforations in the patterns of constellations, and on three walls, at intervals, were tapestries of Persian design. They ordered two Martinis. Gussie lifted her fragile glass at once and took a generous swallow. Then she sat for thirty seconds and looked at the olive.

"Well," she said, "that's that."

"Yes, it is," Donna said, "isn't it?"

"I'm glad he wasn't buried," Gussie said. "What a filthy dismal day it would be to be buried! Do you mind if I'm morbid, darling?"

"Not at all. I'm feeling rather morbid myself."

"I may even get slightly drunk as well, which would only have the effect of making me more morbid. Would you object to that?"

"Whatever you want to do is all right with me, Gussie."

"Thank you kindly, Mistress Mary. That's from a nursery rhyme, you know. That Mistress Mary bit. Do you know why I am thinking of that particular nursery rhyme at this moment? It's because Mary had a garden, and we have a garden, and the question was and is, how the hell does it grow? Well, not so well, I guess. Ours, that is. The garden surely looks like it's going to hell, doesn't it, darling?"

"Maybe not, Gussie."

"Anyhow, never mind. I'm just a filthy morbid woman, and I wish I were dead instead of Aaron, and that's the truth. It's the truth at this time, at any rate, but I admit it may no longer be true tomorrow, or even an hour from now."

She finished her Martini and signified to the waitress that she wanted a second, but after it was brought she sat looking at it sourly, as if she were not sure that she wanted it after all. It was her second at this sitting, but it was far past her second for the day, and she had gone to the chapel with gin on her breath. Not drunk, nor on the other hand quite sober. Just quietly and bitterly fortified by gin.

"I'm glad he wasn't buried," she said again. "It's much too cold and wet a day to be buried."

"Why don't you quit thinking about it?"

"I'd be glad to quit thinking about it if I could, but I can't. It seems to be something I can't control at present. Do you know why that is? It's because I am reminded by association of another person who was put into a hole in a soggy cemetery when I was there, but that was a long time ago, and I was a young girl at the time. This person they put into the hole was a person I was going to marry, but of course after they put him into the hole, it was impossible. His name was Aloysius, which is a name I can't imagine any mother giving to a child. But I called him Al, and I loved him, and what is truly remarkable is that he loved me too."

"Don't say things like that, Gussie. Surely lots of people have loved you."

"I don't think so. At least not in the same way as Al. He was a crazy little son-of-a-bitch, to tell the truth, and he insisted on riding a goddamn motorcycle all over the place at simply incredible speeds. I don't know why he did this, but it seemed as if he had to. Maybe it's the sort of thing a kid has to do if he's named Aloysius. Anyhow, he went too fast around a curve on a gravel road, and he hit too much loose gravel or something, and that was the end of him. At least that's what they figured afterward had happened, and he broke a number of bones, including his neck. It was impossible to patch him up properly for display, so I was unable to see him after it happened, but what I remember most about it now is putting him into a wet hole on a day very much like this one."

Donna looked across the tiny table at the ugly, emaciated woman staring sourly at a Martini as if it were the total distillation of her life in a brittle glass bulb, and she thought that Aaron Burns had surely been in Gussie's life a late and rather distorted recapitulation of this boy who had insisted on riding a motorcycle until he broke his neck at it. For this reason, because Aaron had turned to her and not to Gussie, Donna felt as if she had cheated and betrayed a friend. She knew that this feeling was ridiculous, but it disturbed her just the same, and she didn't know what to say.

"What a rotten thing to happen," she said. "I'm sorry, Gussie."

"Well, it hardly matters any more, and I only mentioned it because of circumstances. It had very little effect on me, except to make me hate motorcycles and wet holes in the ground and sometimes myself and everything in general, and now I think we'd better talk about what is likely to happen to the shop. Do you think it will open again?"

"I don't know. Surely it will open, if only until it's finally disposed of. That will probably be quite a long time off, for there are sure to be a lot of legal things to be settled. I don't know much about such matters."

"Neither do I, and I guess there isn't much use in discussing it at all, so far as that goes. We're sure to be notified of what is expected of us."

"For the present, I should think it is in the hands of Aaron's lawyer, Mr. Joslin. Do you think I should contact him?"

"I doubt it. If he wants to talk with you about anything, he'll let you know. Do you know him?"

"Not well. I've met him a couple of times when I was with Aaron."

"He's a nice guy. He was Aaron's friend, as well as his lawyer, and once I spent a weekend with him at a place that doesn't matter. I thought it would be pretty dull because he's so dry and reserved, but on the weekend he was altogether different, quite gay and charming, and I had a very pleasant time."

Suddenly Gussie picked up her glass and drained it of the second Martini, as if it were something she had decided to get down quickly after considering it all this time. After setting her glass down empty, she stood up.

"I don't believe I'll stay and get slightly drunk after all," she said. "I believe that I'll go home and get thoroughly drunk instead. Would you care to come along and join me in the project?"

"I don't think so, Gussie. Thanks, anyhow. I'll stay and have another Martini, if you don't mind, and then I may go to the shop and try to work. I guess there would be no objection to my going to the shop now."

"Why should there be? You still have your key, and no one's fired you yet. Call me if you learn anything, will you, darling?"

"All right, Gussie. I'll call."

Gussie left, and Donna ordered another Martini and drank it slowly. She didn't actually feel like working, and did not, moreover, want to be alone in the shop where she had been so much. On the other hand, she did not want to go alone to her apartment, which was the only other alternative. So she continued to sit at the tiny table and nurse her drink, and when it was finally gone, she ordered and nursed another. This one, too, was gone after a while, and she was left with the choice of ordering still another or leaving. She would have preferred to stay, but she decided that she had better not. So she got up and went outside on the street and waited for a taxi to come along. While she waited, she still hesitated between the shop and her apartment, but once in a taxi she decided abruptly to go home.

In the apartment, looking at herself in the long mirror of the dressing table, she thought that the dress she was wearing was one that Aaron would have liked. When she had passed by his casket, he had looked remote and unreal and utterly unlike anyone who had ever happened in her life, but now, thinking of him without seeing his gray husk, he was credible again and completely believable. She wondered where he really was, where he had gone off to so precipitately from the hall of his house, or if he had simply ceased to function or to exist in any conscious way. She had a feeling that she could at that moment, by making herself inwardly and outwardly utterly still, establish contact of some kind with him. She tried intensely to accomplish this, standing immobile before the glass that no longer reflected her image in the black dress, but there was only silence and stillness. After a while there was a stir and a sigh, and sound and motion resumed: nothing now was clear that had been obscure, nothing now was known that was not known before. Her mirror image returned, and she considered changing into something else, but at that moment the telephone rang in the living room.

The voice that responded to hers was dry and precise, and careful with syllables.

"Miss Buchanan?"

"Yes."

"This is Earl Joslin speaking. Mr. Burns' lawyer. I should like to see you at your earliest convenience."

"Today?"

"It it's convenient."

"What do you want to see me about?"

"I'd prefer to tell you when I see you, if you don't mind."

"I see. Do you want me to come to your office?"

"I'm not in my office now and would rather not go there. May I call on you for a few minutes at your apartment?"

"Yes, of course. I'd be pleased to have you."

"Very well, then. In about an hour, I'd say."

It had naturally occurred to Donna that Aaron might have left her something in his will, and she supposed that it was about this that Joslin was coming. She did not imagine that the bequest, if there was one, would be large, and she honestly hoped that it wasn't, not because she was troubled by any sensibility to higher morality, but simply because a large bequest would be embarrassing and would suggest a relationship she would rather not have known. She would not be seriously troubled whether the bequest was large or small, but what did trouble her seriously was the shop and its disposition and the threat to the beautiful beginning she had made there.

She put some recordings on the phonograph, selections from *Swan Lake,* and again decided against a drink. Earl Joslin would probably accept one when he came, and she would join him. Sitting in the brocaded chair, she listened to the music of Tchaikovsky, and stared at a Van Gogh reproduction on the wall. Responding to the bright sound and color of two tortured minds, she was suddenly reminded of the poet Villon, and of the boy named Enos Simon who had told her about the poet and whom she had neither seen nor thought of for a long, long time. Why, she wondered, did so much beauty come from darkness and despair, and what had ever become of Enos Simon? Tchaikovsky was a dark and distorted man, as were Van Gogh and Villon. Yet the world had received from them a legacy of beauty such as few men leave. Enos Simon would almost certainly not leave from his life a residue of anything, but she wondered where he was and what he was doing and thought for the first time since the fall that he'd left that she would like to see him again.

Having moved backward in her mind, she did not return until the recordings played out and she got up to reverse them. She had no sooner done this than the buzzer sounded, and she opened the door to Earl Joslin, slim and gray and dryly impeccable, who stood waiting at the threshhold. Seeing him there, she recalled immediately Gussie's reference to a weekend, and she found the idea incredible, something she could not imagine. But Gussie had not dated it, and so perhaps it had happened long ago.

"Good evening," she said. "Come in, please."

"Good evening, Miss Buchanan."

He smiled slightly and stepped past her into the room. The smile had a kind of pale clarity, like winter's sunlight, somehow oblique and from a source far off. She took his hat and topcoat and carried them into the bedroom and returned to find him standing near the phonograph with his head canted in a posture of listening.

"Do you like Tchaikovsky?" he said.

"I don't know. The *Swan Lake* score, at least. I know very little about music, really."

"It's very nice, very buoyant. When I was younger, I preferred the heavy things, the *Pathetique* and the odd Beethovens and things of that sort, but as I grow older and heavier myself, I find myself liking the lighter touch. Mozart, I think, is my favorite now. Do you care for Mozart?"

"Not especially, I'm afraid. As I said, I know little about music. I suspect that my judgment is not particularly good."

"Oh, well, perhaps Mozart is for old men trying to forget they're old, although I doubt that such an evaluation would be generally acceptable."

He turned away from the phonograph, repeating his thin smile, and she wagered with herself, watching him, that he was Scotch and soda. She was mildly surprised, therefore, when he said in response to her offer of a drink that he would take bourbon in plain water. She went into the kitchen to fix the drinks, filling his glass from the tap at the sink. When she returned, he was still standing as she had left him, not a perceptible difference in his position or posture. He was, she thought, a remarkably quiet man, deliberate, conservative with sound and motion, as if he practiced a cult of quietude in a world too loud and too agitated. Handing him his drink, she asked him to sit down, and he did so after her.

"I suppose," he said, "you've guessed my reason for coming."

"No." She shook her head. "I thought it would be something about the shop, but I wasn't sure."

"Has it occurred to you that you might have been remembered in his will?"

"Yes, but I haven't thought much about it one way or another."

"I'm happy to say that he left you ten thousand dollars."

"Ten thousand! That's quite a lot of money."

She looked down at her glass, feeling in her breast a sudden clot of pain at this post-mortem evidence of his generosity, a savage resurgence of self-reproach that she had deserted his body in death.

"On the contrary, I think that it's not as much as he really would have liked you to have." Earl Joslin sipped bourbon and water and looked at her quietly over the rim of the glass. "How well did you know Aaron, Miss Buchanan?"

"Quite well. He was my friend as well as my employer."

"Yes. I knew that, of course, without asking. I was his friend, too, besides being his lawyer, and I always enjoyed his confidence. He valued highly not only his personal relationship with you, but also your business relationship. He considered you an extremely talented and clever young woman. This is something you are aware of, naturally."

"I think so. He always implied as much, though he never said it directly. It was unnecessary for him to say it."

"Yes. The best relationships are those in which things are understood. Possessing, as you did, this understanding, were you aware that his private life was not particularly happy?"

"I was aware that he did not love his wife, if that's what you mean."

"Precisely. Please excuse the deviousness that my training has given me. And yet, not loving his wife, he left her, with the exception of your bequest and a small one to Miss Ingram, all of a very large estate, which is much more than the law requires. Do you understand why he would do such a thing?"

"No. I haven't thought about it."

"If you were to think about it now, could you understand?"

"I think he must have considered it a kind of moral obligation."

"True. I can see that your relationship with him was really quite sensitive. As for me, however, I would call it penance." He drank again from his glass and sat for a few moments in silence, either waiting for her comment, if she had one, or considering how to continue. "Aaron Burns was a lonely man," he said. "He was really more than that. He was a tortured man. All his life he was emotionally vulnerable because of the heritage he had rejected. He married for reasons that had nothing to do with love, and the marriage was a great mistake. Afterward he looked upon his wife as a kind of merited punishment and upon his life with her as a kind of penance. To have treated her in his will otherwise than he did would have seemed to him like an evasion of the penance he thought just. It would have been like trying to cheat Yahweh. Do you understand what I am trying to say?"

"I understand what you are trying to say, but I don't understand why you are saying it."

"Well, neither do I, precisely. Let's just say that I am troubled by the memory of this man. Therefore it's a relief to talk about him with someone he loved. Is that a satisfactory reason?"

"Yes. I'm sorry if I sounded rude."

"No. Nothing of the sort. Perhaps I should not have spoken so freely."

"I'm glad you did."

"Good. Then no one is offended. Tell me, Miss Buchanan, are you prepared to continue in your present position at the shop?"

"Yes, but I've been wondering if I would be asked."

"I'm asking you now. I talked with Mrs. Burns this afternoon after the services, and she agrees that the shop should remain open until it is finally disposed of."

"Is it going to be sold?"

"Yes. That is what Mrs. Burns wishes."

"I'm sorry to hear it."

"So am I, frankly. Would you like to know what I advised her to do?"

"Yes."

"I advised her to keep the shop and put it under your management."

"I'm flattered and very grateful."

"There's no need to be. I'm convinced that you are perfectly competent, which precludes flattery, and I was unable to get my advice accepted, which makes gratitude excessive."

"Nevertheless, I am grateful to you for trying. Do you think it would do any good if I were to talk with Mrs. Burns?"

"No, I do not. In fact, I'm afraid it would be unpleasant for you to attempt it."

"I'd be willing to risk the unpleasantness if there were the slightest chance of success."

"I predict that there's more than a risk of the former and less than a chance of the latter. However, you are perfectly free to see her if you please. If you do, I wish you luck."

"Thank you. Will you have another drink?"

"No. I think not. It has been very nice talking with you, but now I had better go."

He stood up, and she stood also. Taking his empty glass, she set it with her own on a table and went into the bedroom for his coat and hat. Returning, she found that he had walked to the door in her absence, and he took the coat and hat from her and stood with the coat draped over one arm and the hat held in his hand.

"Goodby, Miss Buchanan," he said. "Since I am temporarily in charge of Aaron's estate, it is certain that we'll meet again."

"I hope so."

"Thank you for seeing me."

"On the contrary, I am grateful to you for coming."

4

There was, after the reopening of the shop, an appreciable increase of interest in Donna Buchanan originals. It was real and discernible and tremendously exhilarating. Stimulated by this, and needing in the difficult aftermath of Aaron's death the relief and defense of intense activity, she entered a period of creativeness in which ideas were conceived and executed with a hot facility and perfection. And in her mind she began to evolve the plan for a show, an exclusive presentation of original gowns to those who would come by invitation. The only oppression was the threat of the shop's disposal, and every day she resolved to go to see Aaron's widow. But this was something she dreaded exorbitantly. Every day she postponed it until the day following, and the day never arrived.

In the third week, Queen Hattie returned and asked for Donna. With her was her husband, William Walter Tyler himself. He sat in a chair with his knees crossed and his hat in his lap while Hattie modeled for his approval (after Serena had modeled it for hers) a gold lamé sheath which Donna had designed. Tyler liked the gown and Hattie bought it.

When they were ready to leave, Tyler took Donna's hand and held it for a moment in both of his. It was a gesture of mild intimacy that surprised her a little but did not offend her.

"I greatly admired the last gown my wife bought here," he said. "You have a fine talent, Miss Buchanan."

He said this with an odd wistfulness which was as surprising as his gesture in taking her hand, and she had a feeling that he was suggesting a genuine regret that his devotion to his wife was restricted in expression to the admiration of her gowns. But this, she thought, was really ridiculous, an impression based on preconceptions that were probably not valid. He had certainly meant to suggest that to a strange woman he had only met.

"Thank you," she said. "You are kind to say so, but Mrs. Tyler certainly made the gown appear at its very best."

"That's true," he said. "She's a lovely woman."

And now in Tyler's voice, she would have sworn, the odd wistfulness was effaced by an odd, impatient anger, but this too must have been no more than a peculiarity of inflection that implied what it did not intend. Saying goodby, he turned away and followed his wife out of the shop.

The next morning, compelled by an inexplicable urgency that surmounted her dread, Donna called Aaron's widow from the shop and was given permission to see her at three o'clock that afternoon.

The sense of urgency was the result of an unreasoned conviction that she had reached a particular point in time, a brief period that was psychologically propitious, that she would succeed today in what she would have failed at yesterday or would fail at tomorrow. There was as little validity in the conviction as in the priestcraft of the zodiac, but it sustained her, through the morning and the afternoon, to the time when she was in a taxi and on her way. Then, in the taxi, the hysterical assurance drained from her at once, leaving her hollow and spent and assured of defeat. She compelled herself to complete the errand because it was something she had to do.

When she reached the house, she was let into the hall by a woman she had never seen before but who she suspected was not Mrs. Cassidy. She was younger and wore a white dress that buttoned down the front, suggesting the effect of a uniform. Donna assumed at once, and correctly, that she was a practical nurse Shirley Burns had hired to serve roughly the same purpose a placebo would serve. She offered to take Donna's coat, which Donna retained, and then went out of the hall on rubber soles, leaving her alone in the hall where Aaron had died. How long ago? Only three weeks, plus a few days. And where, precisely, had he fallen and died and lain? A step or two from the foot of the stairs. A little to the left of them. There, right there, on polished oak that bore no stain or scar or any kind of sign, though it seemed, somehow, that it should have. Struck by the idea that if she went and stood on the exact spot she might establish the contact she had tried and failed to establish in her apartment, she went and stood on it. But there was no more this time than there had been the other time. She was still standing there when the woman returned and told her Shirley Burns was ready to see her.

Shirley Burns was sitting in a high-backed chair with a small lamp burning on a table beside her. A book was turned face down in her lap, and she did not rise nor invite Donna to sit.

"Miss Buchanan?" she said. "Yes," Donna said.

"Why have you come to see me? I am not well, and I'd appreciate it if you would be brief."

"I've come to speak with you about the shop."

"What about it?"

"I understand that you plan to sell it. I want to urge you not to do it."

"Indeed? In what way do you consider yourself privileged to interfere with my plans?"

"If I give you that impression, I'm sorry. I admit that I have a selfish motive in wanting the shop to continue as it is, but it would also be profitable to you."

"So I have been told by Mr. Joslin. I repeat to you what I said to him, that I do not wish to be bound to this city by any interests at all. I intend to settle my affairs and leave as soon as possible. However, assuming for the moment that I keep the shop, am I to understand that you are suggesting that I put the operation of it into your hands?"

"That's my idea, yes."

"Why should I do such a thing?"

"Because I am competent and can contribute more to its success than any other person. Your husband knew this to be true, and Mr. Joslin knows it now. I'm sure he would be glad to recommend me if you were to ask him."

"It is unnecessary to ask him, for he has already volunteered that information. Apparently, Miss Buchanan, you made quite a strong impression upon my husband and his lawyer. Especially upon my husband."

"I believe that we understood and respected each other."

"Certainly he must have valued you quite highly. You have been informed, of course, that he left you ten thousand dollars."

"Yes. He was considerate and generous, and I'm grateful."

"Perhaps your gratitude is not altogether necessary. I feel certain that his generosity was no more than posthumous payment for yours."

"What do you mean?"

"You know perfectly well what I mean. Do you wish me to say it directly? Do you think I am such a fool that I don't understand the bequest was payment for the use of your body? I wish you to understand, whatever you call yourself, or were called by my husband when he was alive, that he has made you appear in the end no more than a common whore, which is exactly what you are."

Once before in her life Donna had felt as she felt now. The time had been that late-May night when her father had violated the illusion of a fragment of time. In fury, with a physical feeling of cold, but calm, almost detached in her apparent reaction, she looked at Shirley Burns, as she had looked that other time at her father, with revulsion and scorn that excluded hate.

"I am as willing as you to speak frankly," she said. "I am willing to tell you directly that Aaron and I slept together many times. We did so frequently in this very house, and I have walked through your room and despised you for an inadequate woman without the brains or passion or guts to hold a man who was worth holding. You did your best to destroy him, but I saved him, at least some part of him, and for this you hate me. As for me, I consider hate an extravagant concession that you are not worth. I only despise you, as Aaron did, and am sickened by you, as Aaron was. I regret I came here, and now I am going. And you can go to hell—if you can find one worse than the one you've made."

She turned and walked to the door and out into the hall, leaving the door standing open behind her, and she was followed by the whispered epithet of the woman she left.

"Whore," Shirley Burns whispered after her. "Whore, whore, whore!"

From her apartment, she called the shop and talked to Gussie. "Will you take care of closing, Gussie?" she said.

"Where are you now?" Gussie said.

"At the apartment."

"How did it go with Mrs. Bitch?"

"Badly. There's no hope there."

"Well, that's tough, but you'll remember I predicted it."

"I remember, and I really didn't expect to accomplish much myself, but I thought it ought to be tried."

"What now?"

"I don't know. Perhaps nothing. I'll think about it."

"Sure, darling. You think about it. Goodby, now."

"Goodby, Gussie. See you in the morning."

She began to wonder what she could possibly do with the rest of the afternoon and the long night to come. She was still protected by a sense of detachment, but she realized it would not last, that she must—and quickly— find support. And the support she needed was one which, at the moment, she lacked, a man and the reassurance of a man, a man to talk with if not to sleep with, a man to use if not to love.

She wanted Aaron, but Aaron was dead—if he were not dead, she would not now be in excessive need. Because she had been faithful, in infidelity, she was now alone. While she was trying to decide what to do, the telephone rang. It was Earl Joslin. She thought she heard, after his voice saying hello, the sound of a chuckle, like a dry crackling in the wire.

"How are you feeling?" he said. "Quite well," she said. "Why do you ask?"

"I think you must have just gone through a rather trying experience."

"Oh. With Mrs. Burns, you mean. Apparently she lost no time in calling you."

"When it comes to registering complaints, Mrs. Burns never loses time. I've never known her to be quite so furious before, however. You must have ticked her off pretty thoroughly."

"I confess that I used poor judgment."

"Well, that's in how you look at it. As for me, I'm not so sure. You probably understand, of course, that she's demanding your immediate dismissal."

"Am I to take it, then, that this is notice?"

"Not at all. I'd merely like to talk with you. Is it possible for you to see me this evening?"

"Yes."

"Would you consider having dinner with me?"

"I'd be happy to. Thank you very much."

"Good, good. I'll come for you about eight. Is that acceptable?"

"Perfectly. I'll be ready."

"Until eight, then. In the meantime, I shouldn't worry too much if I were you."

After hanging up, she looked at her watch and saw that it was exactly five o'clock. Her present problem, then, was reduced to the expenditure of three hours, and she tried to think what she could do that would be a defense against her increasing sense of disaster and the concommitant threat of depression. She had reached, she felt, a state of suspension in which she was impotent, a body without energy. She was more than ever by her feeling of impotence irrationally convinced that she had reached a time of enormous significance, that she must now in the matter of the shop, which was somehow identically the matter of her life, succeed enormously or fail definitively.

She mixed a much-needed drink in the kitchen, and stood leaning against the cabinet, feeling inside her the diffusion of the drink's warmth, and reviewing in her mind the selection of gowns that were hanging in her closet in the bedroom. Without knowing exactly the reason, or trying to know it, she felt compelled to make on her dinner date with Earl Joslin the best possible appearance. This need was stronger and more directed than the natural desire of a woman to make the most of her assets, but it was not concerned specifically with the effect she might have on Joslin himself. What it surely was, though she didn't verbalize it or even recognize it, was a reaction of pride and defiance to the threat of devaluation.

The decision made regarding the gown, she did not think of it again. She finished her drink and rinsed the glass and went back through the living room and into the bedroom. Moving with a deliberateness that was imposed to kill time and secure serenity, she undressed and lay down on the bed and closed her eyes. If only she could make her mind impermeable to all ideas and images, she would be able to go to sleep, but it would be necessary to awaken by seven, at the latest, in order to be ready for Joslin when he came. She began telling herself that now she would sleep and would awaken at seven precisely, for she had heard that this was a kind of control to which the mind was actually subject. Whether or not this was true, she did go to sleep after a short while and did awaken at approximately seven. She got up at once and bathed and fixed her fingernails and face and brushed her hair and dressed. She was looking at herself in the mirror and thinking that the silk taffeta had been a wise choice when the buzzer sounded. She went to the door and admitted Earl Joslin into the living room.

"Good evening," he said. "Do you mind if I say that you're looking particularly lovely?"

"On the contrary," she said, "I would mind if you didn't. Do you want to leave at once, or would you prefer to have a drink first?"

"Perhaps it would be as well to have a drink after we get there. I thought we might go some place not too elaborate. A quiet place that permits conversation. Do you agree?"

"Yes. I'd like that."

She got her coat, and they went down to the street where he had left his car, a black Chrysler Imperial. He drove neither slowly nor excessively fast, but with the same precise conservatism with which he apparently did everything, regardless of the degree of its significance, and they reached the restaurant he had chosen within half an hour. He let her out at the entrance and drove around the corner to park the car and was back after a few minutes. Inside, in an L-shaped dining room, they sat with approximately nine square feet of snowy linen between them, a candle burning in a frosted column in the center of the linen. A little to her left was a small combo—a piano, guitar, bass fiddle, and drums—that played a variety of rhythms, mostly Latin American, and played all of them softly. In the soft light, hearing the soft rhythms, she felt somewhat relaxed and less imperiled, and his presence across the table, his thin gray face and suggestion of surety, contributed also to the relief of depression. But despite all this, the light and the music and him, she retained the insistent sense of crisis which she could not lose. She picked up her menu and glanced at it and put it down again, feeling suddenly that even the nominal task of choosing among appetizers and entrees and salads was a burden too heavy to assume.

"I would like a Martini," she said.

"Good. I'll have one too. Would you prefer that I order dinner for both of us?"

"Yes, please."

He studied the menu while the waiter was getting the Martinis, ordering quickly when the waiter returned. She lifted her fragile glass and let some of the Martini slip down her throat; it was dry and strong and did her good.

"I won't ask you what you said to Shirley Burns this afternoon," he said. "I'll only comment that it must have been most effective."

"I'm sorry that it turned out as it did," she said. "I went there to try to influence her to keep the shop and let me manage it, but I was not very successful."

"That was apparent. I believe I warned you that she wouldn't be receptive to the idea."

"Yes, you did. It was something, however, I felt I had to try."

"I can understand that. As I said earlier on the telephone, you are to continue in your present position so long as I am in control of Aaron's estate. If you still want to, that is."

"Yes. I want to stay on for the present."

"Have you considered what you will do when the shop is sold?"

"I've been trying to think, but I've been unable to come to any decision."

"Perhaps there will still be a place for you under the new owner, whoever it may be."

"I've considered that too, but I don't feel I should depend on it."

"No. You're right there. It doesn't pay to anticipate these things."

He drank some of his Maritini. Then placing the glass on the table, he laced the fingers of his hands above the glass in an odd kind of pose.

"Have you thought of trying to acquire the shop for yourself?" he said.

"I've thought of it, but I don't see how I could manage it. I estimate that it will sell for around two hundred thousand dollars, which is to me an incredible amount of money."

"Your estimate is pretty accurate, certainly, and it's a very large amount of money to anyone. Well, I only mention this as a possibility, although a remote one, because I am convinced from Aaron's comments and my own observation that you could make a big thing of it. The initial investment, I concede, is a problem. If you decide, however, to try to swing it, I suggest that you talk with Bill Tyler at the Security Bank and Trust Company. He is a client of mine, and I would be glad to speak to him in your favor."

"Thank you. You are very kind."

"Not at all. I believe you have real talent and could make a success of the business, that's all. Or perhaps that's not entirely all, either. The truth is, I like you very much—as Aaron did—and I would like to see you do as well as he wanted you to do."

She looked down at her folded hands in her lap, presenting in the posture an effect of demureness that seemed to him all the more appealing because she usually appeared so deliberately sophisticated. To his generosity she felt an intensity of gratitude that clotted her throat and choked her. When the feeling had diminished, her throat clearing so that her breath passed through it easily again, she looked up from her hands and smiled.

"You see? Regardless of what you say, it returns to kindness. You are under no obligation at all to be concerned about me."

"All right. It doesn't matter. Let's just say that my concern, whatever the basis, is genuine, and I would like to help you if I can. Do you think you could handle a loan sufficiently large to buy the shop?"

"I'm sure that I could successfully pay it off in a reasonable time, if that's what you mean, but I don't see why anyone should accept my confidence as security for so much money."

"Have you no security besides your talent and your confidence?"

"No. I own nothing except my personal things, which are of little value."

"You could mortgage the shop itself, of course."

"Would that be sufficient? I know so little about these things."

"Ordinarily it wouldn't, I'm afraid. However, if you could impress Bill Tyler as favorably as you have impressed Aaron and me, it might. I doubt that he would risk bank funds in that amount, but he has a large personal fortune, you know."

"You mean he might be willing to loan me the money personally on a mortgage?"

"If you can convince him that it's a good investment. There's another angle, too, that I've thought of. He might be willing to buy the shop himself and put it under your management. Much the same sort of arrangement you wanted Shirley Burns to agree to. This wouldn't be as big a thing for you, but it would possibly be more appealing to him because he'd stand to make a much larger profit than interest on a loan."

"I see. I hadn't thought of that. Do you suppose he would be interested? Why do you suggest Mr. Tyler?"

"It would be up to you to make him interested, with what help I can give. I have suggested him because I know him well, because he's a millionaire who can afford to consider such investments, and because he has the kind of imagination that just might be intrigued by a different sort of venture like this."

She looked down at her hands again. Now it was excitement instead of gratitude that she felt, but it had the identical effect of clotting her throat and making it difficult and a little painful to breathe. Before she could look up and respond, the waiter arrived with their dinners. She was glad to see he had ordered capon, which she liked, for she was conscious all at once of being much hungrier than she had realized. His thoughtfulness and wisdom in anticipating her hunger seemed to be, on top of everything else, another subtle claim upon her. They began to eat and to talk of other things, when they talked at all. A few minutes before ten, while they waited for coffee, he looked at his watch and said he had a telephone call to make. Excusing himself, he went away, and she sat and watched him go, wondering idly, without real interest, whom the call would be to—a client or a friend or his wife. Then she realized that she did not even know if he had a wife or not, and had not even thought to find out. The combo finished one number and began another, and the one they began seemed quite familiar, something she should recognize. She followed the rhythm and tried to identify it, but she could not. Then a voice spoke her name at her shoulder, and the voice sounded as familiar as the music, something she should also recognize, but couldn't. She looked up at the face of a young man, a rather handsome young man with dark and slightly curly hair, and the conviction of familiarity remained. Then, when he smiled in a hesitant way that seemed to suggest an inner uncertainty regarding his welcome, she recognized him, with an emotional reaction which she would not have expected and for which she was in no way prepared. She had not thought to see him again, and had felt no desire to see him again, but now seeing him, she could not understand why she had been so indifferent.

"Enos Simon," she said, and held out a hand.

He took her hand and bent over it slightly, and his smile widened and strengthened and gained assurance.

"Hello, Donna," he said. "Did you have trouble remembering me? If you hadn't, I was going to kick you under the table as a reminder."

"I confess that I had trouble for a moment. You must admit, however, that you have reappeared rather suddenly. Won't you sit down?"

"No, thanks. I know that you are with someone. The truth is, I've been watching you for at least half an hour. Earl Joslin, isn't it? You must be doing well for yourself these days."

"I met him through my work, and he has become my friend. I'm sure he would be happy to have you join us."

"I am with someone myself and can only stay a minute. I've thought of you often, Donna. It's wonderful seeing you again."

"I have often thought of you too," she lied. "Are you living here again?"

"Yes. I came back in January of this year."

"That long ago? Why haven't you looked me up? Are you married?"

"No, I'm not married. Actually, I don't quite know why I haven't tried to see you before. Perhaps I was afraid you would not want me to. I wouldn't want to presume on something that happened when we were little more than kids."

"Oh, nonsense. I'd like to talk with you and learn what's happened to you."

"Well, it covers quite a bit of time and takes a while to tell. More than we have now, at any rate. May I see you again?"

"If you like."

"When?"

"Suppose you suggest a time."

He stood looking down at her, and she felt in him again, as if it were a tangible substance that projected and touched her, the kind of intermediate mood she had felt in him frequently during the summer after she had graduated from high school. He was, somehow, both withdrawn and supplicating, expressing mutely an appeal he feared would be rejected, and she remembered suddenly that he had openly expressed his dread of rejection more than once. It was really impossible, she thought, after so many years to read so much into an expression, a hesitation, hardly anything at all. But she felt it anyhow, as she had before, and responded to it now, as she had then.

"I suppose you will not be free later?"

"No." She shook her head. "I think we had better make it another night."

She actually regretted that it was impossible, or at least impolitic, to let him come to her apartment later. And she tried to make this regret plain in the inflection of her voice. But she could see immediately that he reacted in the way she did not wish, with a kind of morbid and unreasonable sensitivity, as if he had been repulsed in a totally improper advance.

"Well, it doesn't matter, there's no hurry about it," he said. "Perhaps it would be better if I were just to give you a ring sometime."

"Yes," she said, "perhaps it would."

He nodded and went away without saying goodby, and she began to wonder why she had responded so warmly to someone she had hardly missed, and would not have missed if he had never turned up again. Now that he had returned so abruptly after his long absence, however, she was honestly anxious to see him, to talk with him and to learn what he had been doing in the interim between going and coming. There seemed to be no good reason why she should be so involved and she couldn't understand why. But it did not have to be understood, so far as that went, because it was something that could simply be accepted.

Just as all things, she thought, must be accepted in the end for what they are and without concern for how they became—the inexplicable allegiance, for instance, of a man like Earl Joslin, who was legally and morally uncommitted and who was now coming back to her among the tables.

5

She was alone in her apartment and in bed by eleven-thirty, and she thought that she would never go to sleep, though she kept her eyes resolutely closed and tried to make herself as passive as possible. After what must have been a much shorter time than it seemed, she did in fact go to sleep and was awakened at ten minutes after twelve by the sound of the telephone ringing. She assumed, at least, that she had been awakened by the telephone, but she wasn't quite sure. She waited for a repetition of the sound which, when it came again, was the buzzer at the living room door.

She turned on the light and put on her glasses, thereby becoming somehow more capable of coping with such intrusions as bells and buzzers and midnight callers. After waiting for the sound to stop and start again, she got out of bed and slipped a robe on over her transparent blue nightgown and went to the door. The buzzer started for the third time, expressing a kind of angry desperation, clearly transmitting the temper of the caller. She asked herself who could possibly be at the door at such a time, and she answered that it had to be Enos Simon, a certainty she possessed without knowing why. She only knew that it was he, by a kind of sense or insight or premonition that was independent of logic or evidence. So she was not in the least surprised when she opened the door and saw him there in the hall.

He had been drinking, was really quite drunk, and this was a condition she had never seen him in before. He stood looking at her with eyes that expressed the same strange confusion of anger and desperation she had heard in the buzzer. This seemed to her wholly irrational, because she could see no reason why he should be either angry or desperate. His face, she saw now, was much thinner than it used to be, and it looked older and tireder than the intervening years should have made it. At first, right after opening the door, she was angry that he had presumed to come here after she had told him not to come, very late and clearly drunk in addition, but her anger, if it was actually strong enough to be called that, was quickly gone. She understood perfectly well that he had come now, neither earlier nor later, because he was somehow driven and could not help it. She felt strong by comparison but somehow vulnerable.

"You had better come in," she said.

He walked past her into the room and sat down in almost the exact center of the sofa, folding carefully at knees and hips and sitting with a peculiar rigidity of his torso, not touching with his back the back of the sofa. She sat down beside him. Turning his head only slightly, he looked at her from the corners of his eyes with a curious mixture of uncertainty and slyness.

"Are you angry because I've come?" he said.

"No," she said. "For a moment I was, but now I'm not."

"Why? Why aren't you angry?"

"I don't know. I admit that I should be, but I'm not."

"You shouldn't have let me in, you know."

"No doubt you're right. At this hour, I probably should never have answered the door. Nevertheless, I have let you in, and here you are, and I should like to know why you have come."

"That's simple. Because I wanted to see you, and I didn't want to wait any longer."

"Well, I find that difficult to accept. You have been in town since January, you said, and you might have seen me long ago."

"I told you that I was afraid you wouldn't care to see me again. You remember that I don't like to risk rejection. After I saw you tonight, though, it became different. It became intense and near again, as it was that last summer, and I had to come."

He spoke slowly, with slightly exaggerated enunciation. He had been drinking heavily, that much was certain, but he did not speak as if he were drunk, or had even drunk excessively, except for the abnormal caution he was exercising.

"You have had too much to drink," she said.

"Yes, I have. I admit that I have. Having too much is something I do too often, and I admit that also."

"You didn't used to drink at all, except a little beer."

"True. It's something I've learned since then."

"Why do you do it?"

"Well, it comes in handy."

"For what?"

"Oh, for all sorts of things. For forgetting things, and for making things seem different than they are, and for acquiring courage to do things I wouldn't otherwise do."

"Is that why you drank tonight? The last reason?"

"To get the courage to come here? Yes. Of course. There is certainly no point in denying it. I drank quite a lot in quite a short time, and here I am."

"It was completely unnecessary. Now that you're here, I'm very glad to see you."

She said it, she thought, only to reassure him, but after the words were spoken she realized that they were true. She realized also that they should not, for her own good, have been true at all. In her life, he could be at best no more than a mistake, and this kind of mistake at this time was something she could not afford.

"Why are you glad?" he said.

"I don't know. Perhaps I am also remembering how it was that summer."

He turned to face her more directly. Without thinking, she reached out and took one of his hands. "Is that true?" he said.

"I think so. I'm not completely sure. I may know definitely after a while."

"It was good, that summer. It was the best time of my life. Do you know that I was a little afraid of you?"

"Why ever should you have been?"

"Because you were so sure of yourself and I was not. You knew just what you wanted to do, and I hadn't the least idea. Still haven't, for that matter. Are you designing, as you planned?"

"Yes. I'm working in a shop here."

"Are you successful?"

"Somewhat. I'm becoming so, I think."

"You see? You are certain to succeed in anything you choose, and I am just as certain to fail."

"There's no good reason why you should fail. Why do you feel this way?"

"I've tried to understand it, and I believe it is because I do not choose at all. I'm always chosen. Do you see the difference between us? You choose, I am chosen."

"I don't think I see any sense whatever in that."

"Maybe there isn't any."

"What are you doing now?"

"Teaching."

"Here in the city?"

"Yes. At Pine Hill."

"Teaching at such an exclusive school is quite an accomplishment, it seems to me."

"Not at all. It's a horrible place, crawling with detestable little monsters. Every day I think I cannot possibly endure another one."

"Oh, please! It can't be as bad as that."

"It's worse. It's unspeakable, and therefore I don't want to talk about it."

"All right. We won't mention it again. Would you like me to make you some coffee?"

"No, thank you. I don't believe I need any coffee. What I need more than anything else is to go to bed, but what I need least of anything else is to go back to my room at the school, and this puts me in a dilemma. I'm no good in a dilemma. When I'm in a dilemma, I just do nothing or start drinking. That's something else that drinking is handy for that I forgot to mention."

She knew while he was speaking what she would do, and knew also she shouldn't do it. Once, a very long time ago, she had wanted him and had had him briefly. Afterward she had not wanted him in the least, and had been unable to understand why she had ever wanted him. Now, because of her strange vulnerability, she wanted him again, knowing the time would shortly come when she would again *not* want him.

"Would you like to stay here?" she asked.

"I'd like it very much if you will let me."

"It's all right. You can stay if you want to."

He leaned toward her and let his head fall forward upon her shoulder. She put her arms around him and felt, under the thin stuff of her gown, the hot appeal of his hands, to which she responded.

He is lonely and in need of me, she thought, *and I am lonely and in need of him too, though he doesn't know it, and if it is a mistake for one or for both of us, as it will certainly turn out to be, it is at least one that we can now make the most of.*

Disengaging an arm for a moment, she removed her glasses and laid them aside.

CHAPTER V

Thinking severity would be appropriate, she wore a brown wool gabardine suit and a simple white Dacron blouse with a string bow at the collar. As she waited in an outer office for Tyler to become free, Donna wondered that she had bothered to come here on an errand, certainly futile and with small chance of success. But she understood she was compelled to explore all possibilities, however remote, just as she had been compelled to effect the fiasco with Shirley Burns. Two hundred thousand dollars was to her an enormous sum of money, something about which one might talk, as one talked about the light years to the sun, but which was never quite clearly comprehended or obtained. Here in the rich atmosphere of the bank, where money was handled and kept in staggering amounts, paradoxically it seemed to be more remote and unobtainable than ever. However hard she tried to convince herself of the reasonableness of her effort, she simply could not imagine that a shrewd and conservative financier would risk so large an investment in her talent and confidence, which were all that she had to offer as security. Perhaps he would scoff at her. Perhaps, even worse, he would treat her appeal with the kind condescension that one accords the fantasy of a child. She could not bear the thought she was absolutely the greatest possible fool to expose herself to such humiliation, and if she were to leave immediately, she could still avoid it. But she did not leave, of course. Because she was compelled, she sat and waited.

"Mr. Tyler is ready to see you now. Please go right in." Standing, Donna crossed to Tyler's door and let herself into the office. Now that she was irrevocably committed and was acting positively, her dread of the interview was suddenly gone. The first thing she felt inside the office was an extravagant pleasure that she had worn by chance a color that went well with the dark walnut paneling, and she was able, moreover, to be amused by her pleasure as she would have been amused at choosing a hat to match a car. Tyler was seated behind a massive desk, walnut like the paneling, and he stood up as she entered and came around to meet her. Behind him an expanse of Venetian blinds admitted light in a pattern of horizontal bars. He was wearing gray, as he had been the one time she had seen him in the shop, expensive and impeccable, and he held her hand a moment with the same cool, dry touch she had noted then.

"How are you, Miss Buchanan?" he said. "I'm happy to see you again."

"Thank you," she said. "I wasn't certain that you'd remember me."

"You're much too modest. It would be more difficult to forget you than it is to remember you." He indicated a chair beside the desk. "Will you sit down?"

She thanked him again and accepted the chair. Seated again, he offered her a cigarette from a silver box on the desk, leaning forward to light it with a lighter that matched the box. The cigarette was just what she needed. She felt relaxed and durable and, if not confident of success, at least prepared to accept failure.

"Has Mr. Joslin spoken with you?" she asked.

"Yes, he has. About you—and very highly."

"Mr. Joslin has been kind and helpful. I don't know why he should concern himself with my affairs, but I'm thankful that he does. I suppose he explained to you why I asked to see you."

"He did, of course, but I'd like to hear it again from you."

"Well, I don't know how to say it except simply. The shop in which I work, which was left by Aaron Burns as part of his estate, is to be sold. I would like to buy it myself, but I have practically no money and no security. My proposition is that your bank loan me two hundred thousand dollars, which would be secured by a mortgage on the business."

"For better or worse, you have at least put it precisely. I understand from Mr. Joslin that the business has been doing extremely well."

"Yes. It has done well, and I'm certain that it will do even better in the future if I am able to continue along the lines we have established."

"I can easily check the past record of the business, of course, but it is not so easy to verify what may be anticipated. What makes you feel, now that Mr. Burns is dead, that the business will not deteriorate?"

"Because I contributed much to its growth in the past few years."

"That you are exceptionally talented in the designing and execution of fashions I am convinced. There is more to operating a business, however, than the creation of a product. Do you also have the training and the quite different kind of ability that would make you successful in management?"

"I think I have. When Mr. Burns had his second heart attack, I was left in charge. I admit this was for a short period. Nevertheless, it was long enough to give me the feel of things and to assure me that I could have run the shop indefinitely."

Tyler helped himself to a cigarette. He sat quietly for a few seconds, looking down at the glowing ash and the thin ascending silver smoke.

"Two hundred thousand dollars is a lot of money, Miss Buchanan," he said at last. "It is especially a lot of money when it belongs to someone else and is merely in one's custody. What I'm trying to say is, I must exercise a conservatism in the investment of bank funds that I might not exercise in the investment of my own. At any rate, a loan of this kind and size could be made only after a very meticulous investigation, and I must tell you honestly that I can't offer you much reason for optimism. I accept personally your statement about the condition of the business, but you can surely see that you as an individual are an additional and relatively unknown factor of peculiar significance in this case. I am certain, I must tell you, that your request for this loan will not be approved."

She received his judgment with no sense of shock, as if, after all, it was of little importance. Anyhow, nothing had been said that she had not anticipated and been prepared for. Smiling faintly, she stood up.

"In that case, I'll not waste any more of your time. Thank you for being honest with me."

"Please." He lifted a hand and looked at her, and after a moment she sat down again in the chair. "As I indicated previously, I am not always so conservative as an individual as I am as a banker. When Earl Joslin talked with me about this, he suggested two alternatives to a bank loan. One was a personal loan. The other was that I buy the shop myself and let you manage it. I am willing to consider either of these alternatives, but I confess that the latter appeals to me more. If I am to gamble, I want it to be for high stakes, and the profit from the business—if it were to be as successful as both you and Earl expect—would be far in excess of legal interest. I'd have little or no time to devote to the enterprise and would be dependent upon you, on whom I'd be gambling. Would you consider such an arrangement?"

"Yes. Mr. Joslin also suggested that possibility to me. I told him then that I was agreeable, and I still am. The truth is, of course, that I would consider it an extremely good opportunity."

"Good. You understand, I hope, that I'm not committing myself. I'll check thoroughly and consider carefully, and I reserve the right to decide on either the loan or the purchase, or neither."

"That's understood."

"In that case, I'll let you know my decision as soon as possible."

She inferred from this that the interview was at an end. She stood up, and he stood up after her, and she offered her hand again to the cool, dry contact of his.

"You have been very considerate," she said. "Thank you very much."

"Don't thank me yet." He shook his head and smiled. "Perhaps it will come to nothing, and you will have nothing to thank me for. Goodby, Miss Buchanan."

On the street, she felt a singing sense of exhilaration and a lightness of body that made every step seem ludicrously high and long, as if she had to force her feet to earth against a tendency to float. At a corner she paused and considered where she should go and what she should do. If she returned to the shop, she would have to tell Gussie about the interview, and this she did not want to do, not because she did not want Gussie to know, but simply because the exhilaration, the singing sense of good feeling, would surely deaden and dissipate if it were touched by words, and she wanted to hold it as long as she could. She did not, however, want to be alone. She wanted someone with her, someone to talk with and to touch and possibly to love—and the one she wanted, she realized suddenly, was Enos Simon. She would return to her apartment, she thought, and perhaps call the school; and she would walk the long way to her apartment because she was feeling wonderful on a wonderful day and simply preferred walking to riding.

She walked steadily for a long time, but, slowly, as she walked, her euphoria and effervescense diminished as her body tired. By the time she reached the apartment she was depressed, and convinced that she had allowed herself to be deceived by an attempt at kindness, which if it was only that was really cruelty. The more depressed and hopeless she became, the more she wanted someone with her—not just anyone but Enos Simon specifically.

2

William Walter Tyler, behind his desk, sat and watched the pattern of light on the heavy carpet. It was quite still in the room. From the outer office and the bank and the street, no sound penetrated. The horizontal bars had moved a little, a little farther out upon the carpet, and would soon disappear.

He thought with a stirring of quiet bitterness that a man was entitled to a time of peace. After a while, after the passing of so many years, the feelings of hunger and emptiness should pass and leave a man alone. He was forty-eight, and he had thought indeed that he had reached the time that was surely the right of every man—a time if not of peace at least of quiet, if not of fulfillment at least of the absence of nagging desire. Now he knew that such a time had not come to him. He watched the pattern of light, the sign of the sun that rose and set. He remembered a young woman with a restless feeling he should never have felt. A young woman, hardly more than a girl, with a supple body that housed needs he could never meet because it was, for him, simply too late. That is what he told himself, that it was simply too late. But he watched the pattern and did not move, and remembered her face and hands and voice.

He had twice before been disturbed in the way he was now disturbed, once by a child when he was a child, and once by a woman when he was a man. The child had been fifteen; he had loved her; and she had died. She had been, in fact, the cook's daughter, coming now and then to the Tyler home, but he had hardly even spoken to her, because he wasn't allowed to fraternize with servants' children. When she came, she always remained in the kitchen, or in the garden just outside the kitchen door, and she was, he thought, the most beautiful girl he had ever seen. Having been taught by his mother to be a snob, he could not understand why a person of his social position should be so affected by the daughter of a cook. He suffered intensely, as a young boy suffers. Sometimes he lay in bed at night and remembered her as he had seen her in the garden, he thought that his heart would literally burst. It was then that he learned something of the nature of pain, that it was an immensely complex and irrational reaction.

He suffered from loving her, and the suffering was ecstasy, but then she died, and he suffered still, but there was no ecstasy in it any longer. His anguish was secret and somehow shameful, so intense and shattering that it was like a brutal physical violation of his incipient manhood. In his room, he wept. In his heart, he despised himself because by his snobbishness he had deprived himself of a friend, or the more that she might have been. When she was buried, the Tyler family sent a magnificent arrangement of white carnations, and Mr. Tyler, William Walter's father, attended the funeral as the representative of the family.

She died of tetanus. Trying to understand why it was necessary for her to die at all, William Walter saw it in its simplest terms as a mortal conflict between a beautiful girl and a microscopic bug. The bug had been the victor, that was certain, and since he had been taught that God took a personal interest in such matters, he could only assume that God had been on the bug's side. This thought was not original with him. It was something he had heard or read, the effect of a similiar experience related by someone else. It was an intolerable assumption, however, one which he could not accept; neither could he subscribe to the hypocrisy that such things happened for the best in God's design. The truth of it, so far as he could see, was that God was compassionless, remote and unconcerned, if not impotent, and beyond the reach of supplication. This was a belief he always held afterward, the only tenable one in his judgment. The Tylers had been Episcopalians for generations, and he remained an Episcopalian, attending and supporting the church but accepting little that was taught in it.

The second person to disturb him comparably, quite a long time later, was the young woman he married. He met her at a tea dance to which he had gone reluctantly. She was a cousin of his hostess, her house guest, and her name was Harriet Cochran. Her family was wealthy, though not nearly so wealthy as the Tylers; and when he looked at her, he thought of expensive crystal gleaming in candlelight. That was an understandable response to her particular kind of loveliness, for she gave a deceptive impression of cool and detached delicacy. Actually, she was physically strong, and psychically she was both strong and resourceful. William Walter fell in love with her immediately, which was disturbing but not unpleasant, for love is unpleasant only when it is frustrated or dying. She responded to him promptly, with restraint, and was obviously prepared from the beginning to marry him. Their courtship fell just short of formality, all things always in the best of taste; they were united eventually in a grand ceremony and went to Europe on their honeymoon. The union was approved by both families, and everyone considered it especially fortunate.

It wasn't. When they returned from Europe, he had already accepted the truth that he was not married in any real sense at all. This was traumatic, and it reflected favorably on the resiliency of his personality that he was able to adjust to this readily and adequately. At first their failure caused him naturally to wonder and probe and diagnose, but slowly, or really relatively quickly, he became convinced that it was something much better left alone. More than that, it was something that could be vastly disruptive if disturbed. He felt in the beginning defiled and tainted, as well as cheated, but self-devaluation was not natural to him, and the feeling passed. In his public life he remained aggressive, adding to a fortune that was already large, but in his private emotional life he withdrew and became passive, thankful, as the years were used up, for the gradually diminishing demands of his body.

Now after such penury and long oppression, his flesh and spirit were at last awakened and causing him pain. It was strange, he thought, that this could happen so long after he had stopped thinking it possible, and all because of a clever young woman who wore the rather ridiculous kind of glasses that clever young women so often seemed to prefer. She was, moreover and quite obviously, exorbitantly ambitious. He did not criticize her, of course, for being clever or ambitious, for he had himself been both, and still was. What he criticized her for—or at least felt a strange mixture of excitement and resentment for—was her capacity to arouse within him emotions he did not want aroused, and he tried to understand why it was that she could do this.

I have known many women more beautiful, he thought, and the truth is, she is not beautiful at all. She is only quite clever and knows how to make the most of what she has, but this in itself is perhaps as important as beauty is. At any rate, she is more provocative than anyone I have known or can remember seeing, provocative in a deeper and broader sense than is generally meant when the word is used, and there is more in this effect by far than can be explained by the response of certain glands. I was aware of it in the shop when I went there with Harriet, and I remembered it and considered it, and I was more than ever aware of it this afternoon in this office, and I think it is largely explained, apart from her face and body and voice and the deliberate effect she achieves through skill, by her almost childlike dedication to what she must do and be. She is not, however, either cold or narrow, as dedicated people often are, and there is certainly in her a potential for

splendid passion. How I should know this, knowing her so slightly, is some-
thing I do not understand, but there is something else that I understand quite
well, which is that I had better now for the peace of my soul begin to forget
her before it's too late, or more to the point, because it already is.

His thoughts and the silence were suddenly oppressive, and he turned abruptly in his chair and pressed a switch on the intercom.

"Have the attendant bring my car around, please," he said. Leaning back again, he waited a few minutes, giving the attendant time; then he got up and crossed to a closet and put on his hat and coat. Passing through the outer office, he spoke briefly to a woman with a pince-nez and then continued on his way through the bank to the street. His timing was precise, as it almost always was, for the car had just arrived before him. It was a small car, a Chevy, and he knew that it was considered an affectation in a man who could have afforded any kind of car, but it gave him a kind of satisfaction to drive the Chevy, affectation or not, and he got into it now and drove away. Weighing in his mind the alternatives of his town apartment and his house in the country, he decided upon the house in the country, especially since it was Friday and the weekend was ahead. The truth was, however, that neither was a place he fervently wanted to go to. He wondered how long it had been since he had gone any place with fervency. It had certainly been longer than he cared to remember. If he went now to the house in the country, however, he would have to stop first at the apartment to ask Harriet if she would care to go, even though he knew she would stay in town. Nevertheless, it was an obligation to ask, and so he continued in the direction of the apartment and was there in little over half an hour.

In the foyer, he gave his hat and coat to a maid and was told that Harriet was not in. He went through the living room and into the adjoining study. Alone in the room, he mixed a drink and drank it slowly, thinking again of Donna Buchanan and wondering what she was doing at the moment and what she would be doing in the coming three nights and two days. This seemed to be of immense importance—knowing the things she would do and the places she would go, knowing if they would be places and things she really wanted to go and do or if, as in his own case, they would be no more than time-fillers. Would she work? Would she go to a show or go dining or dancing? Did she have a lover, and would she sleep with him? He thought these things, and he realized that he was like a stricken schoolboy. It did him good to think so of himself, and he smiled about it and drank his drink. After a while he heard the voice of Harriet in the living room.

Having finished his drink by then, he mixed another for himself and one for her and carried them out. She had gone directly to her own room, however, and so he followed her there and rapped on the door with the edge of the glass in his right hand. She asked who it was and invited him in when he told her, but he was obliged, because of the glasses, to ask her to open the door from the inside.

"I thought you might like a drink," he said.

"Thank you."

She took the drink and carried it to a table and set it down without tasting it. Carrying his own, he crossed to the bed and sat down on the edge of it. She was really very beautiful, he thought, watching her. She was more beautiful than she had been when he married her, and this was rather remarkable because she was thirty-eight years old now, ten years younger then he. He conceded the beauty and admired it—and was not stirred by it in the least.

"I've decided that I'll drive out to the house," he said.

"Have you? I thought you planned to stay in town."

"I did plan to stay, but I've changed my mind. Would you like to come along?"

"No. It's impossible. I have commitments here."

"Do you object to my going alone?"

"Not at all. Please do just as you like about it."

He lifted his glass and lowered it and sat for a moment looking down into it. "As a matter of fact," he said, "I've been thinking of going away for a while."

"Away? Where?"

"I don't know. Just somewhere for a change. Only for a few days, perhaps a week."

"I see. Perhaps it would be a good idea if you did go. You've been looking rather tired. Are you feeling well?"

"Quite well. I'm neither tired nor ill. Just stale, that's all."

"In that case, a change would undoubtedly do you good."

"Well, I haven't definitely decided. I'll let you know, of course, if I do."

"All right."

He drank again from his glass, and she stood watching him, obviously waiting for him to leave. She wanted to change her clothes, and she did not want to undress in front of him. In all the years they had been married, she had never undressed in front of him or permitted him to see her naked.

"I would like your judgment on something," he said.

"My judgment? On what? Not on a business matter, I hope."

"It is, in a way, as a matter of fact. Something a little out of my line, however. I think your judgment would certainly be of value to me."

"What is it?"

"It has to do with the local shop in which you bought two original gowns. The shop owned by Aaron Burns, who died recently. You'll remember that I was there with you when you bought the second gown."

"Yes, I remember."

"Do you also remember the young lady who designed the gowns?"

"Yes, I remember. Donna Buchanan. She's very talented."

"Do you intend to continue buying gowns from her?"

"Yes, I do. I'm convinced she will build quite a reputation. Why are you so interested?"

"As I said, it's a matter of business. She wants to borrow money to buy the shop, so she can continue to use it as an outlet for her work."

"Then loan it to her. She will certainly be successful."

"As a designer, I have no doubt. But there is more than that to running a successful business."

"Well, that's something I know nothing about."

"It will take at least two hundred thousand dollars. That's quite a lot of money to invest with no more security than the shop itself."

"Surely you don't expect me to advise you regarding your investments."

"Of course not. All I wanted, really, was your opinion of Miss Buchanan's ability."

"I've told you that. She is certain, in my judgment, to go a long way."

"Isn't it rather unusual for a designer to start in this way? Don't they usually get a position with a large outfit, or something of the sort?"

"I suppose they do, usually. I suspect that Miss Buchanan is an unusual person."

"Yes. I suspect that myself." He drained his glass and stood up. "Well," he said, "I think I'll get started for the country."

"All right. I hope you have a pleasant weekend." He went over to her and touched his lips to her cheek and went out.

She undressed and lay down on the bed and began to think about the harpist, another talented young woman, whose expenses she was paying at a local conservatory.

3

Enos Simon walked slowly beneath the pines of Pine Hill. It was four o'clock, and he had survived another day of classes, which was something to be thankful for, but how to survive the day after, or the days after and after and after, was something he could not imagine or even bear to think of. Fortunately, however, it was not necessary to think of it, at least not at the moment, because this was Friday and there were no more classes until Monday. This was something else for which he could, he supposed, be thankful. He walked slowly because he was by no means eager to reach his destination and because he was much more tired than he should have been. But he soon reached the house in which he lived, which was only a short distance from the school, right at the foot of the hill, and inside in his room he stood looking out the window and up the hill in the direction from which he had just come.

He hated the hill and the pines. He would have hated them anyhow, for reasons he would never understand, but he especially hated them because they looked like a hill and pines he had known in another place in another time. The place was not far away, nor the time so very long ago, and from his window there he had looked down the hill instead of up; but otherwise the two views were almost identical. Sometimes *he* had the feeling, looking out the window and up the hill, that the same doctor who had gone to talk with him there would return to talk with him here. He had not hated the doctor, who tried to be kind and helpful, but neither had he wanted to talk with him, always feeling relieved when he went away. One of the reasons he had not wanted to talk was that he would say things about himself that he afterward regretted saying. When he felt this regret he would go back over the conversation in his mind, trying to recall it precisely—and this was disturbing. Quite a long while after he had left the place—especially at times when he was particularly depressed—he would find himself trying to reconstruct one of these conversations. It was impossible, of course, to do this accurately, and the remembered conversation would be a mosaic of bits gathered from many conversations and imagined words that had never actually been said.

"How are you feeling today?" the doctor asked.

He did not feel like talking and remained silent. He wished the doctor would go away.

"Don't you feel like talking?" the doctor said. "Do you want me to leave you alone?"

This was, of course, what he did want, but he could not bring himself to say so, for the doctor meant well and was only trying to be kind and helpful.

"It's just that I don't feel very well," he said.

"I'm sorry to hear that. Do you think I might be able to help you? In what way do you feel bad?"

"Well, in a number of ways, actually. It's rather hard to put your finger on anything specifically. My head aches quite a bit—it's not exactly an ache, more like it's sort of stuffed with something. And I ache in other places too, and feel as if I had a fever."

"I can assure you that you don't have a fever. Your temperature's perfectly normal."

"I didn't say I had a fever. I only said I feel as if I had."

"Oh. I see. Well, is there anything else you would like to tell me about? Is your wrist painful?"

"No. My wrist doesn't bother me at all. That's a very small thing. What bothers me most is the feeling I have that I have come to the end of things."

"To the end of things? What do you mean, to the end of things?"

"Oh, I don't know how I can make it any clearer than that. It's just a premonition or something. As far as I'm concerned, everything is finished."

"I'd be very much interested to know why you feel this way. Would you care to tell me?"

"I don't know. It's hard to say. I've always had this feeling that I'd come to a bad end. It's not something you can just simply explain."

"Do you think you deserve to come to a bad end?"

"I suppose I do. I'm not much good, I guess. I've never been able to do anything of any consequence, and I'm a coward besides. Terrible things have happened to lots of people who were much better than I am."

"I dare say that's true. Terrible things have happened to lots of people who were better than I am, too, but that's not our fault, is it?"

"I don't know about that. I don't know."

"You said you're a coward. I don't believe you are, or at least no more than we all are, but I would like to know what makes you think so. Are you afraid of anything in particular?"

"Right now, you mean?"

"Now or any other time."

"Well, I've thought about it and tried to understand it. Mostly it's only a kind of general feeling, not about anything in particular, but sometimes it attaches itself to something, and then I'll be afraid for a while of whatever it attaches itself to. Later on the feeling will get general again, and then become specific about something different, or maybe the same thing again, and it keeps going on that way."

"What are some of the particular things you have been afraid of?"

"I don't believe I want to talk about them."

"That's too bad. Sometimes if you talk about such things, it helps."

"Well, I don't think it will do any good, but I guess it won't do any harm, either. I was afraid of God once for quite a while, because I thought He was going to do something terrible to me, and I was afraid of people all together, society I mean, and I was afraid of contamination and diseases like epilepsy and such things."

"Are you afraid of God now?"

"No."

"How did you get over being afraid of Him?"

"I quit believing in Him."

"Are you afraid of society or disease?"

"No."

"Are you afraid of anything in particular now?"

"No. Nothing in particular. I just feel that something is wrong with me, with my life, and I don't know what it is except that it is something terrible that I won't ever be able to get rid of. It's something I was born with, I guess."

"Is that why you did what you did to your wrist?"

"Yes, that's why."

"It's really unnecessary and unreasonable to let yourself become so depressed over the things you mentioned, God and society and things like that. Don't you understand that?"

"I understand that it's unreasonable, but I can't help it."

"Of course you can't. I see that, all right. But perhaps we can help you to help it. As you said, these are merely things or ideas to which your depression attaches. Since you understand that, we are already a long way on the road to understanding the rest of it. Well, now, you see? We have made some progress in just this little while, and I believe we have talked enough for the present, don't you?"

The doctor stood up and looked around the room. His eyes discovered and rested upon a book.

"I see you are reading the *Grand Testament,*" he said. "It isn't often you see someone reading Villon. Do you like him?"

"Yes, I like him. He is a fine poet."

"Is that the only reason you like him? Because he is a fine poet?"

"No. I like him because he was an evil man who created a kind of beauty that few good men have been able to create."

"Why does this idea appeal to you? Because you find it reassuring in respect to yourself?"

"I guess so. I'm evil, too. It's something I've felt to be true for as long as I can remember, and I wouldn't have felt it was true for so long if it weren't."

"And it makes you feel a little better to believe that evil people are capable of great good?"

"Great beauty, I said."

"Beauty is good, isn't it?"

"That's right. I guess you're right about that."

"Can't you see that if you were truly evil you would not be concerned about your potential for good?"

"I don't know. It's all part of the same thing. Just twisting words around won't change it."

"Have you ever done an evil thing?"

"That doesn't matter. Doing evil and being evil are different things. God knows the difference."

"I thought you had quit believing in God."

"Oh, well, that's just a manner of speaking. I can see that you are only trying to catch me up, and that's no help to anyone."

The doctor smiled again and placed a hand lightly for a second on Enos Simon's shoulder.

"I said we had talked enough for the present, and here I have started all over again. It's a weakness of mine. Whenever you've had enough of me, you mustn't hesitate to say so. Goodby, now. Perhaps we can talk again soon."

He went away quietly, and Enos Simon looked down at the slope and the pines.

As he now looked up at them. In this different place, at this different time, quite a long while later. His depression was increasing, the deep dark swing of the cycle, inexplicable and inexorable, that never swerved to the antithetical elation, the mania, but hovered only between depression and release from depression. He knew quite well that he should not be standing here in idle submission looking up the slope among the trees, that it was in fact the worst thing he could possibly do. But it was a part of the dark process to want most to do nothing when it was most imperative to do simply anything. It was a mistake also to remember the past, the effects of depressions that had become confused with causes, and he knew quite clearly what a mistake it was. It was one he had made before, and often, but he continued to make it, in spite of his knowledge.

There was, for instance, the time he had gone with a group to a home for incurables; it had been a day depressing in itself, a gray day of cold rain in which the sun had never shone. He had seen these patients, these men and women in all stages of degeneration, some in that terrible corruption of body and mind, and looking at them, he had wondered where their souls had gone. It was easy to believe that a normal person possessed a soul, but where was the soul of an idiot? And what happened to the soul of a person who had once not been an idiot but had become one slowly through degeneration over a period of time? And how could one seriously believe in something that was supposed to be the very essence and immortal part of life and yet was subject to physical corruption, or at least had no discernible existence apart from it in the way that the mind might survive cleanly and discernibly in a body otherwise mutilated? And most terrifying of all, if the soul survived, did it survive an idiot as an idiot soul?

This kind of speculation was very bad for Enos. Afterward he was unable to forget what he had seen or to quit thinking about it in the way he had begun. The depression he felt was far more enduring and intense than the brief and normal depression that would have come to any sensitive person from the visit. It was a morbid malignancy that grew and grew; he became obsessed with the idea that this visit had been a kind of warning of his own destiny, and at the same time he was driven to irrational efforts to avoid the destiny that was preordained. Everything was contaminated, a personal trap. He had only the vaguest ideas of how such debilitating diseases were contracted, but he knew there was no innocence left in the world, that everything had become an agent of contagion, and it required the most stringent effort to eat or drink, or touch so much as the knob of a door. This went on and on, but at last the fear passed. Or, rather, it was exchanged for a different fear which he dwelled on until it also was exchanged for still another. And in between, once in a while, there were interims of uneasy peace.

The chronology was confused in his mind, but of the interims of uneasy peace, one was a period encompassing a spring and a summer, remembered afterward as the time of Donna. Sustained by her, he experienced in those few months the brightest period of his life since the days of his early childhood, and the day after the climax of their relationship, he felt a sense of worth and confidence and a security that their love would survive and sustain him from that time forward. For a while it did sustain him, but then he began to slip from the level of brightness, caught again in another of the dark cycles; and he was certain that she did not love him, as actually she did not, that no one on earth, because he did not merit it, could love him with permanence or any depth. When his parents moved during his first college term, he had already given her up as lost, and himself also, and he did not return to her to suffer the rejection and humiliation which he anticipated with irrational certainty.

He struggled on through college and reached his third year, which was the worst period of all, the worst of his life—and just why it was worst he could never tell. There was no unusual precipitating incident, nothing at all that he could isolate and define. In the depths of unremitting depression, he felt devaluated and impotent and unfit to live; one afternoon, he returned to his room and tried to quit doing what he was plainly unfit to do. In the bathroom, which was shared by other students, he ran the tub about half full of water and held his left arm below the surface and slashed his wrist with a razor blade. He was afraid of the pain in the last moments of living, but there was only an insignificant sensation in the instant of action, and hardly any at all afterward as his blood mixed pinkly with the water.

It was a fine definitive action of which he was proud in the instant of its execution, but it turned out to be, after all, only another failure and humiliation—a climactic rejection of all rejections, no less than the scorn of death itself—for neglecting to lock the bathroom door, he was found, saved and sent away. Then had come the episode of the hill and the pines and the doctor who came to talk; and after that, after a sustained period on the top of the cycle, his release to the business of living for which he was somehow unfit. Because there seemed to be nothing else to do, he returned to the university and finished his course. Eventually, through the good offices of a friend of his father, after a couple of beginnings and failures in other places, he had come to this second hill of pines. Now here he was, looking out the window and up the slope, wondering how he could possibly go on with the intolerable task of survival.

Looking and wondering, he began to think of Donna, who had returned to his life like a kind of incidental miracle, and he felt the lift in darkness thinking of her always brought. He knew he must go to her again at once, with her permission if possible and without it if necessary, as he had gone three times since their first meeting. Stirred out of his perilous lethargy by the thought of her, he turned away from the window, went to the telephone and dialed her number.

In her own place at that moment, with a need far less profound than his, Donna was wanting him.

4

She was awakened suddenly by a sound at midnight. She did not actually know that it was a sound that awakened her, the assumption and acceptance of it simply being in her mind upon awakening, but she knew that it was midnight, because she could see, by turning her head slightly on her pillow, the luminous face of the bedside clock. Her left arm was pinned and numb, but she did not attempt to release it, lying very quietly, instead, and waiting for the repetition of the assumed sound, which very shortly came. It was no wonder that the sound had awakened her, for it was strangely penetrating, in spite of being very soft, and it was, she thought, a kind of whimper, a sound of dumb suffering.

Her arm still pinned, she raised her body from the hips as far as she could and leaned over Enos Simon to look down at his face. On his face was the visible expression of the sound, and as she watched the expression, the oral expression was repeated again, but this time with added shrillness and intensity, and it did not diminish and die away as it had before, but ascended precipitately to a high, thin cry. As if lifted by the force of the cry itself, his body jerked up to a sitting position, her own falling aside to avoid a collision, and the cry ended in his throat with a strangled sound.

"Darling," she said. "Darling, what's the matter?"

He remained in a rigid posture of sitting and did not answer. His body was trembling, but the trembling slowly stopped. At first she could plainly hear him breathing, but then, quite soon, she could hear him only by listening intently.

"You cried out in your sleep," she said. "Did you have a dream?"

"I'm sorry," he said. "I'm sorry I disturbed you." Reaching up, she touched his shoulder, drawing her fingers down his side.

"Lie down," she said. "Lie down."

He lay back slowly, turning to put his arms around her and press his face against her breasts.

"Did you have a dream?" she said again.

"I don't know. I don't remember any dream."

"You sounded as if something were hurting you. Not physically. As if you were suffering."

"Nothing was hurting. I don't know what it was."

"Does it make you happy to be here with me?"

"Yes. It's the only thing. Nothing else makes me happy."

"Did it make you happier earlier? What we did?"

"Yes. Of course. It always makes me happy."

"When it happens, I get the feeling that you are not happy afterward. That maybe you feel it is something you should not do. Do you love me afterward, or do you despise me for a little while?"

"No, no. I never despise you. You only imagine it if you think I do."

"All right. Do you want to go back to sleep?"

"No. I'm wide awake. I couldn't possibly sleep."

"Neither could I. Would you like a drink or some coffee or anything like that?"

"No. I don't think so."

"Or a cigarette? Would you like a cigarette?"

"No. A cigarette is not what I want."

"What is it? What is it that you want?"

"You know. You know."

"All right. All right, darling. All right."

And then, as before, in the achievement of ecstasy and even in the ecstatic accomplishment, she was aware in her bones that it was all a mistake, not in itself alone, but in this way and with this man, and that it might very well be in the end, for him or for her or for both, the worst mistake of all. Afterward, however, lying in the lethargy succeeding excitement, in a warm and delicious indifference to trials and trouble and all consequences whatever, she listened again to his regular breathing, the slow and even pumping of his lungs, and wondered what it was about him that incited her compassion and generosity and almost her love, and she understood suddenly that it was because he was like a child.

He is like a child, she thought, *with a terrible problem, whatever the problem may be.*

"Are you going to sleep now?" she said.

"Maybe now. In a little while."

"Do you feel good?"

"Yes, good. Very good."

"What are you thinking about?"

"You."

"What about me?"

"That you are lovely. That I love you. That I can almost believe in myself when you are with me, and that I cannot believe in myself, and consequently nothing at all, when you are not with me."

"You shouldn't say that. You must not be dependent on me or anyone else. It isn't necessary."

"Don't you think so?"

"Of course not. Just consider a minute. It was only three weeks ago that we met again, and before that we knew each other for only a few months. You see? Out of all your life, you have known me less than half a year, and all the rest of the time you got along perfectly well without me."

"I did not get along perfectly well."

"Nonsense, darling. Certainly you did."

"No. Perhaps sometime I'll tell you just how I did not."

"I'd like that. I'd like you to tell me about yourself."

"Perhaps I'll tell you."

"But not now?"

"No, not now."

"All right. Tell me how things were at school. Did you have a good week?"

"No. I had a terrible week. All weeks are terrible at the school."

"Is it that bad?"

"It's bad enough."

"Why do you stay, then?"

"I don't know. Where else is there to go?"

"I wish you wouldn't talk like that. You sound as if you thought Pine Hill were, so far as you're concerned, the end of the world."

"Perhaps it is. Who knows?"

"Oh, such nonsense! Besides, you are almost criticizing me by implication. I have tried to make you happy, and you obviously are not happy at all."

"You mustn't think that. When I am with you, I am as happy as I can be. I'd like to stay here always."

"That's not possible, of course."

"I could at least stay again tomorrow night. Is that possible?"

"I don't know. I don't think you'd better."

"Why? Can't you stand me two nights in succession?"

"It's not that. It's just that we probably shouldn't do it too often."

"You're only trying to avoid telling me the truth. You simply don't want me. Have you planned to be with someone else?"

"No. With no one."

"Truly?"

"Of course. Do you think I spend all my nights with different men in turn?"

"I'm sorry. I didn't mean that."

"I didn't think you did, really."

"May I stay, then?"

"All right."

"Promise?"

"Yes, I promise."

They lay quietly for several minutes, not talking, and then she sat up and swung her legs over the side of the bed. "Do you want a cigarette now?" she said. "No, thank you."

"I believe I'll have one."

She stood up and walked across the room in darkness to the table where she had left her case and matches. Lighting a cigarette, she stood and smoked it slowly with her back to the bed, and she could hear behind her no slightest sound.

The trouble is, she thought, I *could never be strong enough. I am strong enough for one, but not for two, and after tonight—or tomorrow night, since I promised—I had better send him away for good, before worse is made of what is already bad enough.*

CHAPTER VI

She had planned to go on Sunday to see her mother, but she changed her mind and did not go, and she did not go the following Sunday, either. She tried to convince herself that she did not go because of other things which needed doing, and she actually worked hard at the shop on both days, but she knew quite well, nevertheless, that she did not go simply because she dreaded the visits so much. The third Sunday after her last trip to the high, narrow house on the mean street, she understood that it would be impossible to procrastinate any longer. It had now become imperative to go for the sake of her own peace, if nothing else, and so she took a taxi and got there about three o'clock in the afternoon.

Her father was in the living room. He did not rise from his chair when she entered, and apparently, since there was neither a book nor a newspaper in his hands or near him, he had simply been sitting alone and doing nothing. She was thankful that he remained still and made no effort to greet her physically, for she could not bear to have him touch her. His gray, curly hair was uncombed, and his face below it, still rather handsome in a heavy, florid fashion, had a kind of blurred look, the features somehow indistinct, as if he had been drinking heavily. She knew, however, that he had not, for he never drank at all. Neither did he smoke or gamble or engage in infidelity. His only vices were failure and petulance and sometimes petty sadism. Looking at him, she wished that she might never have to look at him again, but she was determined to be amicable.

"Well," he said, "so you have finally condescended to come and see us."

"I have come to see Mother," she said, violating her amity at once with the pointed exclusion. "Is she here?"

"She's upstairs in bed."

"Taking a nap?"

"I don't know if she's asleep or not. She's sick."

"Sick? What's the matter with her?"

"I don't know. We haven't had a doctor."

"Has she been sick long?"

"Why should you be so concerned? If you came to see her a little more often, or if you lived at home as a decent daughter should, you would not have to ask such questions. What if she had died any time in the past three weeks? Would you want to know how long she had been dead?"

She turned away from him and started toward the door, but when she reached it, she stopped and turned and looked at him with loathing.

"I'll tell you something," she said, "which you know is perfectly true, though you would never admit it. I came here determined to be amicable, but I see that it is impossible, and so I will tell you what we both know. You have done a great deal for Mother, and I have done very little, this is true. But the little I have done has been for good, and the great deal that you have done has been for bad, all for bad. It would have been better if you had gone away and left her long ago."

With an intensification of her loathing, she watched a dull and ugly flush rise slowly into his face. Before he could speak, she went on out into the hall and upstairs to her mother's room. The room was closed tightly and did not look clean. The air was still and sour. On the bed, her mother lay breathing with a harsh, throaty sound, almost as if she were fighting strangulation, and every few seconds the strangled sound of breathing was punctuated by a moan. Crossing to the bed, Donna looked down at the sick woman and saw immediately that she was certainly burning with a high fever. That her illness was serious, if not critical, was obvious. "Mother," Donna said.

She laid a hand on her mother's forehead and repeated the word, and her mother's eyes opened slowly and focused slowly.

"Donna," she said.

She was almost unable to say it at all. The name was hardly more than the shape of the sound with her lips. She lifted a hand above the covers, and Donna caught it as it was falling.

"I'm sick," she said. "I'm so very sick."

Donna had to lean far down in order to hear the words. Besides being faint, they were distorted by pain.

"How do you feel?" Donna said. "In what way do you feel sick?"

"I am cold and hot by turns, and I am sick to my stomach. And my legs and back hurt. I can't understand why my legs and back hurt me so much."

"Why didn't you call me?"

"I didn't want to bother you. I was sure I would begin to feel better soon."

"You should have called me. Surely you know that I want you to call me when you need me. Certainly, at any rate, you should have called a doctor."

"Doctors are expensive. I thought I would get better without it."

"Why didn't Father call one? Damn it to hell, doesn't he have any judgment whatever?"

"You mustn't blame your father, dear. Things are so difficult for him just now."

"Oh, hell! Things are always so difficult for Father. Well, never mind. I'm sorry. You lie still, now, and I'll go call a doctor at once. Would you like the window opened a little before I go? The air is so stale in here."

"If you think so, dear. Only a little, though. I have such chills."

Donna released her mother's hand and crossed to a window, which she lowered about a foot from the top, and then went out and downstairs to the telephone in the hall. She looked up the number of a doctor who had been called to the house before and dialed it with a kind of restrained violence. She was furious with her father for not having called earlier, and the fury was at the same time a useful defense against the guilt she felt herself for having stayed away so long. The doctor agreed to come, and she hung up the telephone and turned to face her father, who had come out of the living room.

"What have you done?" he said.

"I have done what you should have done yourself," she said. "I have called a doctor."

"We don't need you to run our affairs. Your interference is not wanted."

"You would let Mother die without attention, but I will not. I have called a doctor, whose bill I will pay, if that concerns you, and you can go to hell."

"I will not allow you to talk to me like this in my own home. You are not welcome here any longer. Get out of here and don't come back."

"I'll leave your Goddamn house, all right, if that's what you want, but I'll not leave until I've seen the doctor. In the meanwhile, you stay the hell away from me and leave me strictly alone. Do you hear?"

She was certain for a moment that he was going to strike her, something he had not done since that night on the porch when she was fifteen years old, but then he turned abruptly and went back into the living room. She stood and listened while he crossed to his chair and dropped heavily into it, after which she ascended the stairs and entered her mother's room, stopping by the door and staring across at the figure on the bed, which did not move. The sick woman had not gone to sleep, but at least she had become quiet, and it would surely be better not to disturb her until the doctor came. In the meanwhile, it would be quite impossible merely to stand and wait in the shabby, sour room. What was needed was a cigarette, which would be in a measure sustaining and would make time endurable, but it might not be wise to add smoke to the already fetid air in which a sick woman already breathed with a strangled sound.

Stepping back into the hall, leaving the door slightly open behind her, Donna lit the needed cigarette and drew smoke deeply into her lungs. She wondered how long the doctor would be in coming. She hoped that he would not be long, for the last thing she wanted was to stand here waiting and waiting, with guilt and loathing in her heart for herself and her father, and the old ambivalence of contempt and love for her mother, who was very ill and possibly even dying. Perhaps it would be best, after all, if she did die, and perhaps her mother herself thought it would be best and wanted it and for that reason had not called the doctor or expressed any need for one. She had wasted everything—everything was gone and nothing at all of any value was left to waste—and perhaps she simply recognized and accepted that it was time to die.

Leaning against the wall, staring across at the ugly, faded pattern of roses on the wall opposite, she began to remember—in no particular order, without relationship to the chronology of their occurrence—some of the things she had seen and done and been a part of in this house. The sewing machine singing in the room where women came and stood for fittings. The small girl working the treadle with her hands, sometimes in a colored tent of silk or wool or brightly printed cotton. Mrs. Kullen in her corset in a slant of sun, an oddment with downy thighs. Wayne Buchanan saying grace to God and hating God's world for reasons of his own. A dozen scattered fragments of a part of life renounced and outgrown but still in remembrance an oppression and a threat.

Why does that bastard Tyler wait so long? she thought. *Why in God's name doesn't he simply tell me whether he will or will not let me have the money?*

Downstairs, the front door bell rang and stopped ringing and rang again. Moving to the head of the stairs, she looked down into the hall and watched her father come out of the living room and admit the doctor, a short, plump man carrying the black leather bag that was as much the sign of his profession as the caduceus. After an exchange of words, the doctor came up the stairs alone. He had a round face with sharp little eyes in puffs of darkened flesh. As he rose to her level on the stairs, he looked at Donna, and away, and changed the bag from one hand to the other. He gave the impression of being uncertain as to why he had been called, and what might be expected of him now that he had come.

"This way, doctor," Donna said.

She preceded him to the door of her mother's room and opened it and stood aside for him to enter. She did not follow him inside, but remained waiting in the hall, and after a while lit and smoked another cigarette. When the cigarette had burned to a stub, she lit still another from it. The last cigarette was also a stub when the doctor came out into the hall at last. He blinked and rubbed his eyes with his thumb and index finger and shook his head in a way that she interpreted to indicate solemnity.

"She's sick," he said. "Very sick."

"What's the matter with her?"

"Well, it's risky to say on the basis of a cursory examination, but the symptoms seem quite definite. Chills and fever, pain in the legs and back.

Nausea. Frequent and painful urination. I would say, as a tentative diagnosis at least, that pyelitis is strongly indicated."

"Pyelitis? What's that?"

"A kidney infection."

"Should she be in a hospital?"

"Yes. It would be better. I recommend that she be taken immediately."

"Will you make the arrangements?"

"Yes, yes. I'll call and have an ambulance sent. In the meanwhile, perhaps you could pack a few essentials and prepare her to go."

"All right. I'll get her ready while you're calling."

The doctor went down the hall and downstairs to the telephone, and Donna went into her mother's room. She found a small bag in the closet and put into it the articles of clothing and toilet that she thought her mother would need in the hospital. When she had finished doing this, she went over to the bed and looked down at her mother's face.

"You are going to the hospital, Mother," she said.

"I know."

"You will feel better when you are there. They will make you well soon."

The sick woman's eyes closed and remained closed for perhaps thirty seconds and then opened again.

"I will not get well," she said, "but it doesn't matter. I only want to be comfortable, so that I can die peacefully."

"You mustn't say things like that, Mother," Donna said. "We are sending you to get well, and that's what you must do."

But she did not, of course. She died as she had said, and as she wished.

In her apartment, about three o'clock in the morning, Donna received the news from the hospital.

2

It was a dull, wet day. In the night it had rained, and it had rained also early in the morning. Then it had not rained again, though it had threatened constantly to resume, and the sky was a dirty smear. The wind was northwesterly, still cold. Beside the dark hole that had been opened in the earth, the mound of dirt had been covered with white canvas, but at the edges it spilled out thinly, like a brown stain, on grass that was beginning to show the merest sign of green. In a bush of bridal wreath beside a grave, a scarlet bird of some kind sat and cocked its head.

The minister went through the ritual of consignment. His voice was high, nasal, threaded with a thin sound of petulance, as if he were scolding Death as a trespasser, but the petulance was surely only part of the quality of his voice. It was all depressing, and all unnecessary. Everything was finished, everything had been done and said, and all this—the words and gestures and symbolism—was no more than an ugly superfluity that were better omitted. Since it had not been omitted, however, it would at least be only decent, Donna thought, to complete it quickly and without excessive pretension. Life had been rejected, it was as simple as that; and it was now ill-mannered of Life, to say the least, to cling tenaciously to one who had wanted to go, comfortably and peacefully, to hold her now in the dull gray threat of rain and subject her in the end to the last grim measure of prescribed ritual.

Standing beside Donna, Wayne Buchanan began to sob. The sound of his sobbing was shallow and shocking, rattling in his throat like phlegm. All through the ceremony earlier, and during the slow ride to this depressing place, he had sat silent and decorous. She had thought that she would at least be spared a maudlin demonstration (which was more than she had hoped for to start with), but now it seemed that she was not even to be spared this and she must bear after all, in addition to everything else, this intolerable abasement.

How disgusting! she thought. *How absolutely obscene!*

She closed her eyes and bowed her head and waited, and after a while it was over. In the back seat of the black car in which they had come, she sat beside her father, who was now quiet, and returned to her father's house. It was not really necessary for her to go there—she might have gone on to her own place or to the shop or wherever she chose—but she wanted to go for a particular reason. The reason was that she might walk through the house one last time without obligations or bonds or anything at all to keep her or claim her or bring her back again when she was gone. It would be, in its own way, her own ritual.

In front of the house, she got out of the car and went inside and directly upstairs. She walked through the rooms slowly, staying in each one until she felt impelled to move on, trying in each, by making herself very quiet and receptive, to recover the quality it had possessed in the short-lived period of happiness when she was very young, wanting sincerely in the final moments of the final departure to remember these rooms as kindly as she possibly could. The sewing room she saved to the end. Mrs. Kullen was there when she arrived, and remained when she went. Caught in her corset, fixed in light, she survived all others and would never leave.

In the hall below, Wayne Buchanan was standing at the door and looking out through the small glass pane to the street. He turned when she came up behind him. His face was livid and loose on its bones, and he was at that moment, though she didn't know it, more afraid and alone than he had ever been.

"Are you going?" he asked.

"Yes, I'm going."

"Will you come back to see me when you can?"

"No. I hope that I never see you again."

"But—but why?"

"You are not my father and have never been. You are only the man who helped to beget me."

"How can you say such things?"

"Since they are true, they are not difficult to say. Perhaps it is difficult to hear and accept, but that's your problem."

"I have always tried to do my best for my family."

"Do you actually confess that you could have done no better? Anyhow, it does not matter, because it's a damn lie, and you know it very well. You have been mean and petty and cruel, and you have never tried honestly to do a truly generous thing. I was sick of you long ago, and I am sick of you now, but I am willing to do you the courtesy of forgetting you entirely if you will do the same for me." He stepped aside abruptly and opened the door.

3

Because she wanted to restore at once the pattern of life which had been interrupted by her mother's death, she went to the shop. She arrived just before closing time and went through the salon to her workroom. There, she threw herself into a chair and stretched her legs out long in front of her, arching her back, and feeling in calves and thighs the pleasant tension of muscles. She felt liberated, cut loose, in a way exonerated. She did not have any idea of precisely what she had been exonerated of, but she was conscious, nevertheless, of the lifting of an obscure indictment. Corollary with the liberation was a sense of being caught in a quickening current, a conviction that something of significance was going to happen to her, and that the thing to happen would be good. Reacting physically to the spur of her thoughts, she felt in her flesh a kind of tingling resiliency, and she was impelled to laugh aloud.

After a while, Gussie Ingram knocked and entered without waiting for a response. She slouched in a chair and lit one of her interminable cigarettes.

"Well," she said, "how did it go?"

"Miserably. I'm immensely relieved that it's over."

"I hope you don't mind because I wasn't there. I simply cannot endure a funeral."

"Of course not. It would have been completely unnecessary."

"What will your father do now?"

"I don't know. He'll get along, I suppose."

"I was wondering if perhaps you'd move in with him, now that he's alone."

"No. I wouldn't even consider it. My father and I are not compatible."

"Oh? Well, neither were me and mine, so far as that goes. What in God's name is it that makes fathers so frequently impossible?"

"Maybe they aren't. Maybe ours were exceptions. Anyhow, I am feeling too good at present to spoil it by talking of unpleasant things. Do you think it wrong of me to feel good under the circumstances?"

"I have long ago abandoned judging what is wrong or not wrong, darling."

"Well, I was just sitting here feeling free and rather excited. Rather like I used to feel the last day of school when I was a child. As a matter of fact, I have a peculiar notion that something good is about to happen. Do you believe it is possible to have valid premonitions?"

"Oh, God, darling, don't ask me."

"Wasn't it Huxley who defined metaphysics as the art of befuddling oneself methodically?"

"I wouldn't know about that, either. Huxley and I are as incompatible as my old man and I were, but for different reasons."

"Well, to hell with Huxley and metaphysics. Tell me how things went in the shop today."

"Nicely, darling. I sold your red taffeta."

"Really? To whom?"

"Mrs. Christopher Polk, no less."

"Jesus, Gussie, it's impossible for her!"

"I know. Her ass is far too big. Serena modeled it, however, and Serena's ass is neither too big nor too small, but intolerably perfect. The moment Polk saw the taffeta on Serena, she assumed, of course, that it would look the same on her. The vanity of some of these bitches is perfectly incredible."

"It will have to be altered all to hell."

"I know. The seamstress has it upstairs now."

"Oh, well, it's another original sale, anyhow, and everyone will certainly recognize that the gown can't be blamed for Polk's tail. Some day, Gussie, nothing but originals will be sold in this shop. Nothing at all."

"Say, you *are* feeling good, aren't you? Are you withholding information by any chance? Did Tyler tell you something over the telephone to bring on this optimism?"

"Tyler? Telephone? What do you mean?"

"He called earlier this afternoon and left word for you to call him back. There's a memo on the desk in the office. Didn't you see it?"

"No. I'm sorry. I haven't been in the office since I got here."

"Then you'd better go and call him at once."

"In a minute, Gussie. I don't suppose there's any hurry."

Actually, now that the cure for action had been presented, she was oddly reluctant to commit herself. It was not that she dreaded hearing whatever

Tyler had to say, but just the contrary, for she still felt the imminence of something significant and good, of which the call might very well be the beginning. She wanted to savor the expectation for a while, and she decided that she would smoke a cigarette slowly and call Tyler afterward. Lighting the cigarette, she blew out smoke and watched it rise and thin and disappear.

"Did he imply at all what he wants?" she asked.

"No. It wasn't even him personally. It was a woman. His secretary, I suppose. Why don't you call him?"

"I'm going to. Just as soon as I finish my cigarette."

"Well, finish the goddamn thing, will you, darling? I would like to get away from here, if you don't mind, and I'm damned if I'll go before I learn what he wants."

Donna laughed and stood up, bending down to grind the cigarette out in a tray.

"Jesus, Gussie, you're simply a *slave* driver. All right, then. I'll go and call, and afterward we can go out and have a drink together in celebration, or several in mourning."

She went out of the room and across to the office that had been Aaron's and was now, at least for the time being, hers. Gussie had written Tyler's number on the memo pad, and she dialed, leaning with one hip against the desk for the duration of two long rings, after which the voice of Tyler himself came over the wire.

"Hello," he said.

"Hello, Mr. Tyler. This is Donna Buchanan."

"Oh, yes. Miss Buchanan. Did you think I had forgotten you?"

"I was beginning to wonder."

"I assure you that I hadn't. I would like to talk with you again, but it is a little late in the day for it now, perhaps."

"It's not too late for me, if it isn't for you."

"Well, let's see. I'm just preparing to leave here, but I plan to stop for a drink in a small bar I patronize. Would you care to meet me there? We could have a drink together and talk comfortably. Or I could pick you up at the shop, if you prefer."

"That won't be necessary. I'll be happy to meet you."

"Good. Could you make it in, say, half an hour?"

"If it isn't too far. What is the name and address of the place?"

He told her where to come, and she hung up, after saying goodby, and returned to her workroom where Gussie was waiting.

"Did you get him?" Gussie said.

"Yes, I got him. He was still in his office. I have a feeling he was there just waiting for me to call."

"What do we have, a celebration or a wake?"

"Neither, I'm afraid. Do you mind very much if we take a raincheck on it?"

"Oh, God, stood up again! I guess, at my filthy age and in my condition, that it's to be expected."

"I'm sorry, Gussie, truly I am. He asked me to have a drink with him, and I had to agree, of course, under the circumstances. You can understand that."

"Sure, I understand, darling. And never mind the apology. If I had to choose between me and a millionaire, I sure as hell wouldn't consider it much of a problem, you can bet your sweet chastity on that. And speaking of chastity, I wonder why it just happened to come into my mind at this moment as an appropriate allusion. Do you suppose that my female intuition warns me that yours is under seige?"

"Don't be a damn fool, Gussie. This is strictly business."

"Business is what I'm talking about, darling. Your business."

"I doubt that he'd consider it worth two hundred thousand dollars."

"Maybe on a long-term lease he would. Two hundred thousand dollars' worth of business! My God, it would be a career in itself, and it absolutely decimates me to think of it. Oh, hell, darling, I'm just kidding, of course. I wish you luck and all that, and I'll have a drink to it at the earliest opportunity, which should occur not later than ten minutes from now. Before the evening is over, as a matter of fact, I shall probably have as many as a dozen to it."

She stood up and walked out of the room, looking somehow graceful and very smart in spite of her slouch and sharp protrusions, and Donna went into the lavatory and washed her hands and repaired her face. Five minutes later, in the street outside, she caught a taxi and gave the driver the address that Tyler had given her. Ten minutes later than that, in another street, she got out of the taxi in front of the bar.

It was a small bar, tucked in between a book dealer and a florist, which didn't look like much on the outside, and didn't look much more on the inside. And it certainly didn't look like the kind of bar a millionaire would patronize or ask a young woman to meet him in. Standing for a moment just inside the door, while her eyes adjusted to the shadows, she wondered if she could have misunderstood the number or the name of the street, but this wasn't at all likely. And then, she could see Tyler standing and smiling beside a small table in the rear. She went back to him and submitted a hand to his cool, dry touch, and they sat down together at the table, their knees touching for an instant underneath as they settled themselves.

"First," he said, "I'd like to offer my sympathy. I didn't know until I called the shop earlier today that you had lost your mother."

"Thank you," she said, feeling that she should say more but not knowing what it should be.

"Perhaps it was tactless of me to invite you here. I don't wish to intrude."

"Oh, no. It's quite all right."

"I'm glad. The truth is, I was most anxious to see you again. I've been sitting here like a schoolboy anticipating your coming."

"You're very gracious to say so, but I don't believe it, of course."

"Why not?"

"If you had been so anxious to see me, it could have been arranged much sooner. As I've told you, I was beginning to think that you had forgotten me entirely."

"You couldn't have been more wrong. However, here is the waiter for our order. What will you have?"

"I think I'll have a sidecar."

"Sidecar? I haven't had one for ages. It's brandy, isn't it?"

"Yes. Brandy."

"I'll have one with you. Ordinarily I drink only bourbon and water, but I'm not feeling ordinary this evening." He turned to the waiter. "Two sidecars," he said.

The waiter moved over to the bar, which was not many steps away. She thought, looking at Tyler, that he was certainly a man who never felt ordinary at any time, this evening or any other. His face, she decided at first, was the face of an ascetic, which he surely was not, his nose aquiline and his mouth finely fashioned, suggesting sensuality in conflict with the asceticism. Ascetic, as a matter of fact, was not quite the adjective with which to describe his appearance. She sought the proper adjective in her mind and decided that it was sentient. He was a man aware, possibly in some respects, vulnerable. The waiter brought their sidecars, and she sipped hers hungrily, controlling an urge to drink it right down. It was cold and good, the tart liquid accented pleasantly by the sugared rim of the glass.

"Do you know why I waited so long to contact you again?" he said.

"I heard that you were out of town. Mr. Joslin told me."

"So I was. For about ten days. That is not why I waited, however. Or rather, it is, like the waiting itself, part of the effect of the cause."

"I don't follow that, I'm afraid. Anyhow, I assume that it takes quite a long while to decide about making such a loan."

"Frankly, I haven't yet definitely decided about the loan. I'm considering it."

"Is that why you wanted to see me? Just to tell me that you haven't decided?"

"If that had been all I wanted, I could have told you over the telephone. Shall I be perfectly honest with you? I am not incapable of subtlety and indirection when it is necessary, but I have an idea that you would prefer to have me say bluntly what is on my mind."

"Yes, I would prefer that."

"All right. I wanted to see you simply for the pleasure of seeing you, and I waited so long to do it because I wanted it too much."

"Is that being blunt? It sounds rather devious to me."

"I don't think so, and I don't think you think so, either. However, I can be even blunter. I have not met anyone in many years who has interested me as you have. Do you remember the day I came to your shop with Harriet? Afterward, I kept thinking about you and wishing that I might meet you again under different circumstances. Then you came to my office about the loan, and I thought that the second meeting might cure the first, but it didn't. It only accelerated my regression to adolescence. Am I now being too blunt?"

"No, you are not being too blunt, but I can't understand why you should consider it adolescent to be interested in a woman."

"The quality of my interest was adolescent, and still is. If it were not, I could try to seduce you and be done with it. It involves the most exquisite misery and a kind of masochistic passion for bondage. I am much too old to feel so young—so I have waited for the passing of an emotional condition I had thought and hoped I would never feel again, and thought, when it came, that I could never sustain. But it hasn't passed. It hasn't even diminished. Consequently, if I must feel like a schoolboy, I have decided that I can at least react to the feeling like an adult. So I called you, and so we are here drinking sidecars, and how do you feel about it?"

"I feel relaxed and quite flattered, and the sidecars are excellent."

"That strikes me as being an evasion."

"If it is, it is only temporary, to give me time to understand what you are saying. Are you asking me to have an affair with you?"

"Not yet." He smiled and shook his head. "I am only asking you if you would consider giving us an opportunity to decide sensibly, after a while, whether an affair for us would be mutually acceptable."

"Merely to see you and go out with you? Is that what you mean?"

"Yes. In the beginning, no more than a friendly relationship without commitments on either side, so that we can decide later what we want to do."

"It sounds rather bloodless."

"Believe me, I don't feel bloodless. Quite the contrary. I only want, as a regressed adult feeling strangely uncertain in his regression, to be reasonably sure that neither of us makes a mess of things for himself or the other."

"What about your wife? I have a feeling that she wouldn't appreciate such an arrangement, even in the early stage before anything is decided."

He smiled thinly, looking down into the shallow bulb of his glass, which was now empty. She thought that his mouth, after the thin smile left, was distorted briefly by a twist of bitterness, but she couldn't be sure because his face was obscured by the inclination of his head.

"That needn't concern either you or me," he said. "Since I have proposed such an arrangement to you, however, I am rather obligated to assure you that Harriet and I made our own decision and established our own arrangement quite a long, long time ago. It has worked, in a way, and neither of us is likely to disturb it."

As it was with Aaron, she thought. *Probably it develops from different conditions, but in the end it comes to the same default. Is it going to be my part indefinitely to serve as compensation for inadequate wives?*

"All right," she said. "I don't ask you to tell me anything that won't concern me. There is something else, though, that concerns me a great deal, and I am wondering about it."

"What's that?"

"The loan. Does it depend upon my response to your proposal?"

"In other words, am I trying to bribe you? No. I'm not overly scrupulous, but I'm sure that I'm not doing that. Let's put it this way. If we were later to decide to go ahead with this, I'd certainly establish you in the shop. That's assured. If either one or both of us did not decide to go ahead, I might or might not make the loan, or invest in the shop myself. It would depend upon other factors entirely."

"Well, that is clear enough, and it is also fair."

"I've tried to be both, and I'm glad that you think I've succeeded. Do you want some time to consider your answer?"

"No. I have already decided. I won't pretend that I'm offended by your proposal, for the truth is that I feel flattered. I can't see that I have anything to lose from an arrangement that demands no commitments, at least in the beginning, and from which I can withdraw if I choose."

"I see that you have an analytical mind. I'm beginning to be convinced that I would make no mistake, regardless of our personal relationship, in supporting you as a business woman."

"I'm a good designer and a good business woman, and if it comes to it, I'll be a good mistress."

He laughed with genuine pleasure and lifted his empty glass.

"You have ended our discussion perfectly, and anything else would be a detraction. I suggest that we have another sidecar, and go to dinner afterward."

"I agree to the sidecar, but I am not dressed for dinner."

"You are dressed well enough for the place I'll take you. I warn you at the beginning that I patronize only plain places. I drink in this plain place, where the drinks are good, and I eat in a plain place, where the food is good, and I drive a plain Chevrolet car which gets me from one place to another as well as a Cadillac would. By others, these preferences are considered affectations, and I dare say they are."

"Not necessarily. Perhaps they are signs of humility."

"Oh, nonsense. I'm a monstrous egoist, and they are certainly affectations. If I were poor and couldn't afford it, I'd eat and drink in expensive places and drive a Cadillac at least."

"Well, however that may be, I agree to eat with you in a plain place and go there with you in a plain Chevrolet."

He laughed again, again with pleasure, and signaled the waiter, who brought the sidecars. They enjoyed the drinks and the company of each other, and moved on in time to the plain place with good food, where they enjoyed broiled lobster and still the company of each other, and the evening slipped away.

It was not until after eleven o'clock, when he was taking her home, that she remembered Enos Simon, that she was to have seen him that evening. It was by then, of course, far too late to do anything about it.

4

He waited and waited, but she did not come. He had no means of getting into her apartment, and because he could not loiter so long in the hall, he went back downstairs and across the street and waited there in the dark doorway of a tobacco shop. At first he was able to convince himself that she had only been delayed, that she would arrive soon to secure the equilibrium of his tiny personal world which now stood suddenly in precarious balance, but as time passed he was unable to sustain this conviction. Eventually he was as thoroughly convinced that she would not come as he had previously been that she would. It was then a matter of enormous importance to know why she would not come, whether it was the result of something unavoidable which she would regret as much as he, or whether it was deliberate and ominously significant, a brutal indication that she was sick and tired of him and wanted nothing more to do with him. He reasoned that this was surely not so, for there had been no warning of it, no sign or word or slightest withdrawal. It was not possible, surely it was not, for such a monstrous change to occur all at once with no warning whatever. Or had there, perhaps, been signs that he had missed? Thinking back, he began to fancy that such signs had actually been present in her behavior, a reluctance to which he had been blind simply because he chose to be, a general impression that she was making concessions she would have preferred not to make.

She did not come, and after a while he was absolutely converted to the belief in his rejection. He wondered how he had ever been such a fool as to think that it could have ended otherwise, or continued without ending in a life in which everything that was good ended and nothing ever ended that was not. He felt degraded, debased, absurdly threatened, and he felt for her then, standing in the dark doorway watching her dark windows, a virulent and exorbitant hatred because she obviously intended to destroy him. Or, rather, because she was by some kind of mysterious selective process the agent of the dark forces that had been trying to destroy him all his life. He was aware all at once of a repeated harsh sound in the doorway with him, and immediately afterward he was aware that the sounds were in his own throat and were his own involuntary sobs. Lunging out of the doorway, he turned to his right and moved down the sidewalk at a kind of awkward lope, as if he were pursuing something or fleeing from something, both of which were true enough.

He had no goal, or even conscious direction, but he kept in his flight, or pursuit, or both, to darker streets where fewer people walked. And he continued his awkward loping gait in the empirical knowledge, though it was not specifically recognized as such, that there was a balance of sorts to be held in motion that could not be held when motion ceased, that it would require, once he became static, an impossible exertion of will ever to move again. His body was soon wet with sweat, but he went on and on across intersections and around corners and down the dark streets until, after many miles and a long time, he slipped off the edge of a curb and fell on his knees in the gutter. He remained on his knees for almost a minute, and then he stood up slowly. He felt stunned, incredulous that he had done such an idiotic thing, falling in the gutter as if he were drunk, and he realized dully that he must have veered gradually toward the curb without knowing it. His right knee burned, and there was, he saw, a tear in his trousers. Moreover, now that he was not moving, his wet body began to chill. He was exhausted, and it was necessary to find a place to rest. Stepping back onto the sidewalk, he began to walk again, much slower than before, and a couple of blocks farther along the street he came to a bar and entered.

The room was long and narrow, dimly lighted, the bar stretching the length of one side. Tables and chairs were scattered without order or design over a bare floor that had begun to splinter, darkened and greasy from innumerable applications of sweeping compound. Some of the tables were occupied. A man and a woman sat drinking at the bar. Two other women sat drinking pale drinks at the bar alone, separated by an intervening empty stool. The two lone women were wearing cheap evening gowns, short-skirted, that clung to the upper slopes of their breasts, and they were obviously part of the place. Enos sat at the bar and ordered whisky and water. He drank the whisky at a gulp, gagging a little before he could lift the water and wash the taste from his mouth. His body was drying now, and not so chilled. The bartender refilled his glass, and he drank again, only part of the whisky this time, holding his breath after swallowing and washing the taste away at once with the water. The nearer of the two lone women moved down and sat beside him. She was wearing a thick and sickening scent, and he could see, looking sidewise and down from the corners of his eyes, a swell of flesh below the cleavage of her breasts. The gown was pale green and looked like rayon.

"Buy me a drink, honey?" she said.

He did not want to offend her, but neither did he want to buy her a drink or have anything at all to do with her. All he wanted, with an intensity of desire that was almost nauseous, was to be left alone by everyone on earth. Specifically, in his general withdrawal, he wanted the woman to go away, and he told her so with an exorbitantly precise articulation of syllables, as if he were afraid she would not clearly understand him and thereby force him to the monstrous effort of repeating himself. "Go away," he said.

The woman understood him, all right, and for a moment she considered him with eyes reduced to slits of venom. Then she laughed with professional resiliency and laid a hand on his arm in a placating gesture.

"What's the matter, honey? Something bothering you? Lost your best girl or something?"

Her persistence was an affront, her touch a violation, and her remark was unfortunate, to say the least. He reached across his own body and knocked her hand from his arm with a degree of violence that he did not actually intend.

"Go away," he said. "I don't want you here."

The woman sucked in her breath with a hiss, and darkened lids slipped down again like purple bruises over gathering venom. She spat an epithet and slapped like a cat with her claws. He saw the attack from the corners of his eyes, as he had seen her breasts and swell of flesh, and he tried to avoid it, but he was not quick enough, and he felt on his cheek the burning mark of a nail. Down the bar, the woman sitting with the man had twisted on her stool to watch them, and beyond her her escort leaned far forward over the bar with his face turned toward them, split in cruel pleasure by a stained grin. Behind the bar, the bartender began to laugh, a windy expulsion without body. Quickly, neither speaking nor retaliating in any way, Enos got up and left. Laughter behind him grew and followed, and the woman, for good measure, added another epithet.

When he reached the sidewalk, he knew already what it was that he had to do next, but it was necessary to stop at the curb and think, for he did not know exactly where he was in relation to the place to which he wanted to go. It was imperative, he knew now, to return to Donna's apartment. It was not that he hoped to salvage anything of what was surely lost, but only because there was a kind of negative security in establishing definitively that there was nothing to be salvaged, the kind of dark security he had felt in the end that had been no end before the remembered pines.

Moving abruptly, he walked to the corner and read on an iron post the names of the streets. He was able then to orient himself in relation to Donna's apartment, which was an astonishingly long distance away, and he was dully incredulous that he had walked so far. He began to walk in the direction he needed to go, lunging forward again with the awkward, loping gait that carried him with remarkable swiftness over asphalt and concrete; and he reached the doorway in which he had stood before, just as a Chevrolet drove up from the opposite direction and stopped. He stood quietly and watched as Tyler got out and went around the car and opened the door for Donna. He felt within himself the silent, unbearable beat of pain that was somehow coordinated with the beat of his blood but was separate and stronger and not at all the same. In the brick wall of the apartment house light came up where darkness had been, from Donna's windows. Time passed, and Tyler reappeared and drove away, and the time that had passed was no more than ten minutes, though it seemed longer than a night could be. After waiting yet a little longer in the distorted night where time, and all things, were deceptions, he crossed the street and went up to the floor on which Donna's apartment was and pressed the button beside the door.

"For God's sake," Donna said, "what's happened to you?"

She was shocked at his appearance, almost frightened. He wore no hat, and his hair was tousled, as if he had raked his fingers through it in every direction. His clothes were rumpled and stained in spots, his trousers torn at the knee. The side of his face where he had been clawed was smeared with blood and a little swollen. It was perfectly apparent to her that he had been making some kind of fool of himself, and it was quite likely that he had been impelled to do it simply because she had not been at home to meet him. This made her react immediately with compassion and anger, which were ambivalent, which was a kind of reaction she resented strongly because she had had too much of it and wanted no more of it.

"You had better come in," she said.

He walked past her into the room and sat down. Turning away from him, glad for the moment of the necessity for petty action that would delay her facing fully what was now apparent, that she had taken upon herself an intolerable burden and perhaps a greater responsibility than she had imagined, she went into the bathroom and returned with a wet washcloth and a bottle of merthiolate. She cleaned his face and painted the scratch and carried the cloth and the antiseptic back into the bathroom. Returning, she stood and inspected him from a distance of two paces, feet spread and hands on hips, in a posture that seemed to suggest between them a difference of at least two generations.

"Now, then," she said, "please tell me what kind of idiocy you have been up to."

"You weren't here," he said, "and you didn't come, though I waited for a long time, and so I went for a walk and walked for a long way."

"Did you get yourself in such a mess merely by walking?"

"I fell down. I don't quite know how it happened. Somehow or other I slipped off a curb and fell down."

"How did you get your face scratched?"

"A woman did it. I went into a bar, and she wanted me to buy her a drink, and I didn't want to. It made her furious because I didn't want to buy her a drink."

"Jesus Christ, are you completely without any kind of capacity to cope with things? Do you intend to go on forever letting every little emotional disturbance threaten you with ruin?"

"Why weren't you here? You said you'd be, but you weren't."

"I know. I'm sorry. There was something I had to do."

"You were with a man. I was outside, across the street. I saw him bring you home."

"All right. I was out with a man. I'd have told you so, if only you'd given me time. We had some drinks and went to dinner, but it was really a matter of business. This man may loan me the money to buy the shop, which is very important to me. Right now, it is the most important thing that could happen to me."

He did not respond, would not even look at her, and she resisted a compulsion to kneel beside him and hold his head against her breasts. This would have been a concession, she knew, which would not be good in the long run for him, and perhaps be worse for her. It was clear that she must, this night, refuse to carry any further something that had already been carried too far. Now that her life had taken the direction and gained momentum in the last few hours, he was clearly impossible. He was quite incapable of being reasonable or of accepting a simple and undedicated relationship that might have been pleasant for both of them and possible to maintain, and it was practically certain that he would destroy all her chances absolutely if he were allowed to hang on. She had been disturbed all the way home by the fear that he might be waiting in the hall to create a scene in front of Tyler. She did not wish to be unkind—actually she would have preferred not to give him up entirely—but it was essential she act decisively, in spite of her feelings, for the sake of what otherwise might be lost.

She got a straight chair and placed it directly in front of him and sat down and took one of his hands in both of hers.

"I want to talk with you," she said.

"All right."

"Are you listening?"

"Yes, I'm listening."

"You must understand that all this is impossible. Don't you see yourself that it is? For a while it has been all right, and I hope it has even been good for us, something we can remember later without regret. But neither of us is committed or bound to each other, and it will surely be the worse for us from now on if we permit it."

He looked up at her with eyes which were curiously flat.

"Do you mean that you don't want to see me any more?"

"I mean, at least, that I don't want to see you any more in the way that I have been. I don't deny that I wanted it and was largely responsible for it. I admit also that even now I wish it were not necessary to say what I am trying to say, but it will be better for both of us if we do not try to go on any longer."

"Can't I stay tonight?"

"No. Not tonight. Nor any other night."

He drew his hand slowly from hers and looked down at it with his flat eyes, turning it over and over and peering at it intently, inspecting it, it seemed, for marks or stains or some strange sign of contamination. Suddenly, without warning, he folded the fingers into a fist and struck out with the fist savagely, emitting at the same time a hoarse cry of animal anguish.

The blow caught Donna on the side of the head above the ear and knocked her to the floor, the straight chair falling after her. She was stunned for a few moments, blind and deaf, and when she recovered he was already gone. Reaching out for the chair in which he had sat, she pulled herself into it and put her head into her hands and sat quietly for some time.

She was thankful he had struck her. She felt a little better because he had.

CHAPTER VII

She awakened one morning, about three weeks after sending Enos Simon away. Her first thought was of that other morning when she had awakened in the house of Aaron Burns. There were certain things about the two mornings that were the same, but there were other things that were different. She had the feeling now, as she had had then, that it was late and that she would have to get up at once and go to the shop. But that other day had been a Sunday, with no urgency about going anywhere. This morning was Friday and it was necessary to go to the shop, although there was after all, perhaps, no particular urgency. The other morning of awakening had been in early January, and it had been snowing; and this morning was at the end of April, with over a hundred other mornings and awakenings between, and it was a clear day with a bright scrubbed sky which she could see by turning her head on her pillow and looking up through the window of her room. Now, as then, she was a certain kind of person with a certain kind of day ahead of her, but she was a different certain kind of person and the day was a different certain kind of day, for no person is the same when there have been over a hundred days between what they were and are.

She lay quietly on her back, after having looked up through the window at the sky, wondering idly why she had thought of that other morning the first thing this morning. Reasons existed that made the thinking appropriate, but they were reasons not yet known to her. She could think just then of no good reason at all. The reasons which made the memory appropriate on this morning which she did not yet know and therefore could not think of, were that the first day began what this day would end, and that death figured in both in some kind of significant or symbolic relationship to what happened between. It was good, of course, that she did not now know these things and had no way of knowing or anticipating them, for if she had known through premonition, the day would have been destroyed, or at least impaired, in its beginning. Actually, her day was already being injured, even as she awakened and began to think and looked up through her window at the bright scrubbed sky, but she did not know this and would not know it until the day was almost past. From her viewpoint that morning it was a good day, and it was to remain for its duration a good day in which good things happened, or at least in which she got things she wanted.

She thought again about getting up and going to the shop, but she decided to lie quietly a little longer and think about how things had been going—a pleasure because things had been going well. In the first place, after her mother's death, in the release from old ties and old claims, she had entered a phase of extreme fecundity that had sustained itself and was still continuing. Her mind had expanded with fresh conceptions, and she worked with pleasure and intensity for long hours without tiring, and in most of the hours when she was not working or sleeping there was William Walter Tyler, now Bill. From those times, the times she worked and slept, he was excluded, or in the latter excluded himself—from what obscure compulsion on his part to be perfectly fair or absolutely certain she did not know or care—but she could sense clearly when they were together that she had lost no ground in the mild intimacy that had developed. For her part, she found him much more interesting and compatible than she had expected, and she was quite willing to be agreeable in any reasonable way in return for what he offered or could offer if he chose.

Thinking of Tyler, she began after a while to think of Enos Simon. She did not want to think of him, because thinking of him was disturbing, but it was impossible to exclude him from her mind entirely, though she had tried. She had decided then that it was much less disturbing in the long run merely to think of him voluntarily and reasonably, when it was necessary to think of him at all, and so, by admitting him freely to her mind, avoid creating the conflict of keeping him out. In the first few days after the night he struck her and ran from her apartment, she had worried excessively about him because she now understood what she had previously only felt vaguely—that he was quite ill in a frightening sort of way and had been so for a long time, probably even back in that spring and summer they had shared. To be exact, she was not so much worried about him as about herself. This was not because of the violence he had displayed in the final seconds of the night she sent him away, for she did not believe that he had really meant to attack her at all. He had only been lashing out blindly at something, some threat or force that pressed upon him, and she had been at the moment in the way, and that was all. The reason she worried about herself was because of what he might do to *himself*, for if he hurt himself or killed himself, as she now felt was quite possible, it would place upon her, rationally or not, a burden of guilt that was dreadful to consider.

Anticipating this, she had tried to reason it away, to justify herself in relation to him and what had happened between them, and she tried again now, lying in bed and thinking for a while before getting up. What she thought was that she had been kind to him and generous and had at least given him something for some time, and it would certainly be insane of her to blame herself because she had been unable to give him more, when no one else had given him anything at all. This was true enough, but what nullified it and disturbed her was the realization that he would have been better off, much better, if she, like all the others, had given him nothing. There was no sense in this, however, no sense at all, and there was no sense, either, in lying and thinking about it and anticipating something that had not happened—and would surely never happen as a result of anything she had done—now that three weeks had passed. It was a fine day, a spring day with a bright sky, and the sensible thing was to get out of bed at once and start living it.

She walked barefooted through the living room and into the kitchen and put the coffee on, and then walked back into the living room and through it and into the bedroom and from the bedroom into the bathroom. It was a pleasure, a subtle and sensual delight, to feel on the soles of her feet the sequence of sensations incited by the soft looped pile of the bedroom rug and the stiffer clipped pile of the living room carpet and the smooth cool surface of the kitchen linoleum, the same sequence in reverse when she returned, and finally, almost like a tender bruise, the cold and absolutely ungiving bathroom tile. Showering, she remembered again how on that other morning she had walked naked and arrogant through Shirley Burns' room, had showered and later dressed in the inappropriate scarlet sheath, and had finally walked downstairs to discover Aaron dead. This had all happened only a hundred days or so ago, and it was incredible that it had been no longer, and that so much had happened, and was still happening, since that time.

But she was thinking again of the day that had happened instead of the day that was happening; this accomplished nothing and was likely, besides, to become depressing. So she turned off the shower and toweled herself vigorously and returned to the bedroom. Retrieving her glasses from the bedside table where she had laid them last night, she put them on, the first act of dressing, then she stood for a minute before her mirror and smiled at herself and received a smile back. There was in this a kind of renewal, as if she had been bored and had met unexpectedly someone she had known and found stimulating and had almost forgotten; and with the renewal of pleasure there was also a renewal of the old resolve, that nothing should be wasted or lost before it was used, not talent or training or time or the fortunate arrangement and quality of flesh and bones. Now, however, that other morning kept intruding upon this morning, actually seemed to keep repeating itself in small parts removed from the whole. She was, for an instant before she moved, looking at herself in another mirror in another house three months ago, and everything that had occurred since would have to be repeated just as her image was now repeated in glass. Moving away from the glass and out of the glass, she dressed and fixed her face and went back to the kitchen where the coffee was ready.

Sitting at the tiny kitchen table with the coffee hot and black in its cup before her, she began for the first time to plan the day precisely around the things that were already established. There were two appointments, one in the morning and the other in the afternoon, with two women who wanted gowns designed for specific occasions. It would be necessary to listen to their ideas and then modify them, or transform them completely to conform with her own which were already definite and partially on paper, and this was a delicate process requiring time and tact but which would mean at least a thousand dollars between the two of them and possibly even more. It would also be necessary to talk with Earl Joslin regarding the business, since it was still owned by Shirley Burns for whom Joslin acted, but this would be, because everything was going so well at the shop, no more than a routine conference. It would be, besides, a pleasure to talk with Joslin, who had been kind and helpful from the beginning, and still was. In the beginning, as a matter of fact, she had thought that he was possibly motivated by something more than kindness and a genuine respect for her ability and had expected him to make eventually some kind of overt bid for concession. She had wondered how she would respond if he did, but he had never made it and now quite palpably never would. She was thankful for this, especially since things had developed as they had with Tyler, and it was with Tyler, now that she had reached him in her mind, that the day she was planning would end, in this apartment in whatever development of their relationship he determined or succumbed to. But between now and then there were all these other things to do, and it was certainly time that she started to do them.

She finished her coffee and started. It was the day that ended what the other day had begun, which was, in its simplest terms, her struggle for the shop but was really far more complex, and it was—until long after dark after she had returned to her apartment—a good day that went well.

2

There were some boys down on the slope beneath the pines. From his position in the headmaster's office, by looking over the headmaster's left shoulder and through the bright glass pane of the window behind him, Enos could see them quite clearly. They didn't seem to be doing much of anything in particular, just moving around rather slowly and aimlessly, in and out of light and shadow as they were cast in pattern by the pines and the sun. There was no special order or purpose in their movements, that was certain, and chances were that they had merely walked down the slope to loiter under the pines because it was a good place to go and be on a fine, bright day. The odd thing about them was that they no longer seemed to be the intolerable monsters of a monstrous world, and there was about them, in fact, a kind of halcyon air, motion and grace without the slightest sound. One of the boys had very pale hair; when he moved into the sun the hair changed instantly into white fire, and when he moved back into shade the fire went out as instantly as it had begun. This was very fascinating to see, and seemed for a moment to have some kind of significance that never became clear. The sight of the boys was not at all upsetting to Enos, and this was something different, a change that was part of his new peace. This was because the boys were now in a different world from his; they belonged to a world which he had left for the last time and to which he would never return, but into which he could still look over the left shoulder of the headmaster through a pane of bright glass.

"Do you understand what I have been saying?" the headmaster said.

"Yes," Enos said. "Yes, I understand."

What he understood was that the headmaster was trying to be kind and firm at the same time, which is standard procedure for headmasters in dealing with both students and young masters. This was something for which Enos should have been thankful, but he was not. The truth was, the firm kindness was more than a little patronizing, or at least it seemed so to Enos, and he was offended by it, because he was now, after a long time, superior and invulnerable and in no need of kindness or patronage or anything at all from anyone on earth. This feeling of detached invulnerability was so strong in him that he thought it must surely be apparent to any sentient person, and he could not understand why the headmaster was not aware of it and persisted in his foolish attitude, as if it were he who were the stronger of the two. But then, of course, when you stopped to consider it, that was because the headmaster was really a dull and inadequate little man who was aware of practically nothing and was more to be tolerated than resented. He was a frail man, with a tracery of fine blue veins visible under his skin; and his hair was white and soft and rather sparse and seemed to float in a kind of detached thin cloud around the contour of his skull. His lower lip sometimes began to tremble, which gave him the appearance of being on the verge of tears, but actually this was only a sort of tic; when it happened he would pinch the lip between the thumb and index finger of his right hand, and after a bit the trembling would stop.

"I regret the necessity for this action very much," he said.

"It's all right," Enos said. "It's perfectly all right."

"If it were only that your instruction was weak, your techniques, or something of that sort, we could undoubtedly work it out. It is not only that, however, as I have tried to make clear. It is that you have lost control of the boys, which means, to be blunt, that you have lost their respect. This is a much more serious matter. Irremediable, I should say. Once you have lost control, nothing is left but to try to start again in another position. I realize, of course, that you have a contract for the remainder of the year, and the contract will be honored, that is, you will continue to receive your salary. However, for the good of the school, as well as for your own, we must remove you from the classroom."

"I don't care about the contract," Enos said. "You can forget it."

"Nothing of the sort." The headmaster shook his head and frowned slightly, as if his word and honor had somehow been questioned. "The contract is binding."

The headmaster was silent, staring at Enos across the desk. His lower lip began to tremble, and he took it gently between the thumb and index finger and pinched, gradually increasing the pressure until it became quite painful. Enos looked over the headmaster's shoulder and through the pane of glass at the group of boys on the slope beneath the pines. The boy with pale hair crossed a path of light, from shade to shade. The white fire flared briefly and instantly died.

A shadow of irritation drifted into the pastel blue eyes of the headmaster as he began to understand finally that the situation was really quite abnormal. It was surely only appropriate that a young master facing failure and dismissal should betray some signs of distress, perhaps even plead for another chance, which the headmaster would have been willing to grant, but Enos seemed quite withdrawn and untouched. And as a matter of fact there seemed to be in him a feeling of deep and quiet relief, a profound thankfulness that circumstances had reached their present point of development. What the headmaster resented more than anything else, though he did not concede it even to himself, was the uneasy feeling that he had himself been maneuvered, through a distortion of normal values that he had not followed and could not understand, into a position of subordination. This was intolerable, forcing him to feel the distress that Enos should in all decency have been feeling, and he was forced to exercise careful control of his voice to prevent his resentment from becoming apparent.

"I have an impression that you are, perhaps, not well," he said. "Have you consulted a doctor?"

"No, I haven't seen a doctor."

Enos continued to look through the glass into the remote bright world of the boys under the pines, and he thought of the other pines and of the doctor who had been in the place where the pines were. But now the remembrance did not distress him, for he knew that he would not be compelled to see that doctor again, or any other doctor, and that he was finally through with all such things, with doctors and boys and pines and schools and all distressing things. There were some words that expressed it very well, the words of a poem he had once read, words about one balm for many fevers, but he couldn't remember them exactly. Anyhow, it did not matter, and it was, under the circumstances, clearly a ridiculous waste of time to sit here any longer in this room with this inadequate little man who was obviously quite determined to make a great deal out of what was, after all, very little.

He stood up abruptly and said, "I'm quite well, there's no need at all to see a doctor. If you have said all to me that you want to say, I'd like very much to go."

The headmaster's lower lip began to tremble again, and he pinched it severely. He did not trust himself to speak and was actually so weakened by a sense of shock that he did not, for the moment, trust himself to rise from his chair. He merely nodded his head and continued to pinch his lip. He remained sitting in the same position for quite a long time after Enos was gone, resenting with unusual bitterness the young master's pre-emptory attitude. Always afterward, thinking back, he remembered his resentment and was ashamed of it.

Outside, Enos walked down the slope. He walked across the grass and under the trees into the remote and halcyon world at which he had been looking a few minutes earlier, and it was as if the glass were still there, bright and shining and wonderfully protective between him and the world in which he walked and of which he was no part in any real sense. When he came to the boys beneath the pines, several of them looked at him and quickly away, but one of them spoke and said "Good afternoon, Mr. Simon." He nodded and said "Good afternoon" in a perfectly normal voice, and he knew that they were watching him from behind and were certainly sorry for the part they had played in what had happened to him. But this did not matter to him at all, not in the least, except that he was truly a little amused that they presumed to pity him. He felt very good, remarkably light in a way that could almost be called effervescent, and as he walked in this remarkably light way, hardly bending the grass beneath his feet, he thought of a pleasant little tune and began to whistle it softly. And he kept whistling it over and over until he came to the house at the foot of the slope in which he lived.

He went inside and upstairs into his room, and when he was there he went directly across to the window that looked out upon the slope which he had just descended. He stood looking out the window and up the slope at the boys, who were still there beneath the pines, and he began to whistle again the little tune that had got into his head and was very pleasant to listen to. After a while he began to get tired—there was quite an ache in his legs from standing so long without moving—so he got an easy chair and pushed it up to the window and sat down. During all this he continued to whistle the little tune. Eventually he stopped whistling for a few minutes, but he missed it so much, there was such an emptiness without it, that he picked it up again and went on with it. The shade got deeper and deeper on the slope outside, which was the east side of the hill, and the boys walked up the slope and over the crest and were gone.

Pretty soon after that, with the shade getting deeper and the boys gone, he began to think of Donna, of the things they had done together and would never do again, and it was not painful, as it had been before, to think of her. This was also part of the new peace that had come with the acceptance of a very simple solution to everything. As a matter of fact, far from being painful, it was now quite pleasant to think of her; it gave him something to do while he sat in the chair and looked up at the darkening slope. He conceded that she had been very kind, and he was grateful for the kindness and wished that he had not struck her—a very bad thing to have done. If it were possible, he would certainly go back and tell her that he was sorry, but it was clearly not possible. What he had better do instead was to write her a note and tell her how sorry and grateful he was, and that everything would be all right from now on. Thinking about writing the note, he became so absorbed in the problem, whether to do it or not, that he forgot to continue whistling and this time did not even miss it.

In time he came to the conclusion that the note should surely be written, that it was no more than the simplest courtesy which was also an obligation. He got up to write it, but it was too dark; this necessitated turning on a light which he was reluctant to do. It was, altogether, another problem which had to be considered, and he stood in the darkness with his back to the window and thought about it. Because he felt he could not shirk the obligation, he eventually walked across the room and turned on a light and sat down at his desk and began to think about what he should write.

It was necessary and very difficult, he thought, to achieve the right tone. He did not want to be tedious, but neither did he want to be excessively curt, which might be interpreted as a sign of anger or accusation. It seemed best on the whole to write merely what he had been thinking, that he was sorry for what he had done and grateful for what she had given, and so he wrote this as simply as he could on a sheet of paper. Then he folded the paper and put it into an envelope and wrote Donna's name on the outside of the envelope. Leaving the envelope on the desk, he turned off the light and went back to the chair at the window and sat down and looked out at the pines on the slope. But now, after the writing of the note, he was beset by impatience that developed from a feeling that he had reached a point of completion, that there was nothing more of consequence to do or see or think, and that he was only wasting time inexcusably. The house around him seemed very quiet, and even as he sat and listened to the silence, it was broken by the sound of footsteps in the hall and a sudden knocking on his door. He turned his head and looked over his shoulder toward the door, but otherwise he did not move, and in a few seconds the knocking was repeated, and he still did not move or speak. He knew very well that the knocker was the other master who lived in the house, a fellow named Calkins. It was dinner time, and Calkins was starting up the hill to the dining room, and he wanted to know if Enos cared to go with him—and Enos didn't. After the second knocking, the footsteps receded in the hall and died on the stairs, and shortly thereafter, looking out the window again, Enos could see the figure of the master ascending the darkening slope. It was then, indeed, time to end delay.

Getting up, he removed his coat and tie and rolled the sleeves of his white shirt above his elbows. He did this in a leisurely way, folding up the sleeves neatly, as if there were some sort of pleasure in the simple act. Afterward, he walked across the room, which was now quite dark, to the dresser. From the top drawer of the dresser he took his safety razor, a small gold instrument which had been given to him as a gift, at Christmas or a birthday or some time, by someone he could not exactly remember, his father or mother, a cousin or someone. Carrying the razor, he went out into the hall and down to the bathroom and inside. He locked the door behind him and snapped on the light and laid the razor on the lavatory and turned on the water in the tub and sat quietly on the commode until the tub was almost full. Then he turned off the water and removed the bright double-edged blade from the razor and stood for several minutes looking at the tub and thinking.

He was not concerned about pain, for he remembered from the first time, the abortive time, that there was very little. Primarily, he wondered about the best position to assume, and he wished that there were a low stool available so that he could sit comfortably. A kneeling position seemed to be the only one that would serve, and so he got down on his knees beside the tub. At the same time, without being aware that he was doing it, he began to whistle the pleasant little tune again. Kneeling and whistling, he submerged both fore-arms in the water with the palm of his left hand turned up and the palm of his right hand turned down. With the small blade in his right hand, he opened the artery in his left wrist. And as he remembered it from the time before, there was only the slightest burning sensation.

A thin red ribbon rose in the water from his wrist and diffused and darkened the water around, and the water grew slowly darker and darker, and the darkness spread from the water over everything, and he died kneeling in the darkness.

3

At five-thirty, Tyler called.

"I'm relieved to find you still there," he said. "I was afraid you might have gone."

"No, I'm still working," Donna said. "I'll be here for at least another hour."

"Have you had a good day?"

"Yes. Everything has gone well. I'm looking forward to seeing you tonight, of course."

"Well, that's what I'm calling about. Something has developed to prevent my coming. It's a nuisance, I know, but I simply can't avoid it."

"I'm sorry."

He was silent for a moment, and she could hear faintly in the background the lilting sound of music—strings and brass and reeds forming the light and perishable pattern of a popular tune. She listened to the tune and liked it and was able to name it. *Lisbon Antigua.* A jukebox. She wondered if he was calling from the small bar to which she had first gone to meet him and where she still frequently met him. She was sure that he was there, and she could suddenly see and feel the place as truly as if she were there, and she wished that she were. Without forewarning, with the faint and perishable tune on the wire between them, it was quite abruptly an instant of crisis, a point from which her life would move inexorably one way or another, and she felt in the instant a surge of panic. He was calling to put an end to things. Already, she was certain, he had simply gone away, leaving the wire open to the inconsequential tune as a kind of commentary on the inconsequential affair he had initiated and tolerated and was now ending, for his own reasons, in this contemptuous manner.

"Are you there?" she said.

"Yes," he said, "I'm here."

"Are you at our bar?"

"Yes. How did you know?"

"I can hear music. *Lisbon Antigua.* "

"Oh. I see. There's a fellow here who seems to like it. He insists on playing it over and over. Would you like me to explain why I can't come tonight?"

"If you want to."

"It would be easier if you were here. Can you come for a drink, or does that work have to be done immediately?"

"It can wait."

"Shall I have a drink ready for you?"

"A Martini, please."

"All right. I'll be expecting you."

She hung up and went out into the salon. Gussie was standing at the rear alone, a cigarette hanging loosely from her lips and leaking smoke in a thin ascending wisp. She spoke without removing the cigarette, squinting through the smoke.

"Leaving, darling?" she said.

"Yes."

"Tyler again?"

"Yes. I'm meeting him for a drink."

"How are things going?"

"About the loan?"

"Yes, of course, darling. Did you think I was being inquisitive about your sex life?"

"I think it may work out all right, Gussie."

"Well, it seems to me that it's taking a hell of a long time. Why don't you simply tell him to crap or get off the pot?"

Donna laughed. She loved Gussie and was never offended by what she said, and she knew quite well that Gussie's vulgarities were a kind of derision directed toward her own sentimentality.

"I'm afraid he might get off," she said.

"Sure. I can see where that would leave us, all right. Right up that well-known creek without a paddle. Do you think this joint is really worth the trouble?"

"Yes, I think so."

"I guess it is, at that. For you, anyhow."

"It takes time, Gussie. We have to be patient."

"I know, I know. I'm just a sour bitch, and you mustn't pay the least attention to me. I think I need a hobby or something. You know. Something to take my mind off things after hours. Isn't that a hell of a confession for a woman to make? Time was I had an entertaining hobby that just came naturally, but I'm getting too old for it. But then, no one wants what I haven't got any longer, so it comes out even in the end. Maybe I'll buy myself a motorcycle."

"You'd better buy yourself a drink."

"That's a superfluous suggestion, darling. Buying myself a drink is something that still comes naturally, and something for which, apparently, one does not become too old. However, thank you for reminding me. Run along, darling, and have fun. I'll finish up here and get out myself in a few minutes."

"All right, Gussie. Goodby, now."

She went out and caught a taxi and went to the bar between the books and the flowers, and Tyler was waiting for her, and so, as he'd promised, was the Martini. The man who liked *Lisbon Antigua* was still playing it—probably it had associations for him. He stood leaning against the jukebox and listened to the music and thought about the associations, whatever they were. At the small table with Tyler, Donna lifted her glass and drank from it and set it down again, and Tyler took and held her hand. And her recent panic and sense of crisis, the irrational reaction on the telephone, was instantly and properly reduced to absurdity.

"I'm glad you could come," he said.

"You only had to ask," she said.

"I want to explain why I must break our date."

"It isn't necessary to explain."

"Anyhow, I would like to. It's nothing much, really. Merely that I must drive my wife to the airport."

"Oh? Is she going away?"

"Yes. For quite a long time. The truth is, she is going to Europe."

"Did she decide so suddenly to go so far?"

He shook his head. "No. It has been planned for some time, of course. Originally, she intended to leave next week, but she decided all at once to leave earlier in order to have an extra week in New York before sailing."

"Is she going alone?"

"No." He looked down at her hand in his, and his voice went curiously flat. "She is going with a friend. Of hers, not ours. Perhaps it would be more accurate to call her a protégée. A young woman who is studying music at the local conservatory. A harpist, I believe. The primary purpose of the trip, I'm told, is to give her training and experience abroad. Harriet is very generous in such matters. Anyhow, it seems that I am expected to drive her to the airport, though I should think a servant would do as well. Perhaps it is merely something a husband is required to do when his wife goes to Europe."

"It's all right, of course. There's nothing else you can do."

"I'd much prefer keeping our date."

"Will it be too late after the plane leaves?"

"It will be quite late. Midnight, I suspect, before I could get back to your apartment."

"That's all right if you want to come."

"Would it be all right if I wanted to stay?"

"You're imposing a condition, and so I won't answer. If you want to stay, you must ask me directly, and I'll give you a direct answer."

"All right. So far as I'm concerned, the preliminary period we agreed upon is over. I want to stay, and I am asking you directly if I may."

"Are you sure it's what you want? Do you remember what it commits you to?"

"The shop, you mean?" He smiled and lifted her hand to his lips in an obviously warm and spontaneous gesture that elicited in her a response of tenderness that she had not felt for him before. "I had decided long ago that you should have your shop in any event. Did I neglect to tell you that?"

"I'm afraid you did."

"Perhaps I should not be telling you now."

"Why?"

"That should be apparent. I'm not the most astute man in the world, but neither am I naive. I am well aware that the shop has been from the beginning my principal negotiable asset. Perhaps my only one."

"No. In the beginning it may have been your only one, but now it is not."

"Nevertheless, since you know that you are going to get anyway what you set out to get, I may have weakened my position."

"You could always change your mind about the shop."

"No. Like most men with few virtues, I make great issue of the few. I don't break my promises, and I promise that you shall have your shop. Now will you give me the direct answer to my direct question?"

"You may stay, of course."

"Because you're grateful?"

"Not only that."

"Good enough. I'm wise enough not to press it any further. And now it's time I was leaving, and I wish it weren't." He lifted her hand to his lips in a repetition of the warm gesture. "Would you like me to take you some place?"

"No, thank you. If you don't mind, I think I'll have one more drink before leaving."

"In that case, I'll see you tonight."

He went away, and she watched him go, and she continued to feel for him the new tenderness that seemed to have nothing to do with his generosity. The man in the rear of the bar kept playing *Lisbon Antigua;* she ordered another Martini and sat drinking it, and she thought that it was really very strange how things eventually culminated so quietly, for better or for worse. She had schemed for the shop and had felt intensely that the shop was absolutely essential to all that she wanted to do and be, that failure to acquire it would somehow be a disaster from which she could never recover completely. Now that she was successful and had achieved all that she wanted through her own efforts and the exploitation of herself, she should have been filled with tremendous excitement and satisfaction, but instead she was only quiet and acceptant of things as they had turned out. She knew that she would have been the same way, exactly the same way, if they had turned out bad instead of good. But she also knew that this was something that would change, that she was now caught in a kind of recuperative lethargy in which she would gather again her emotional energy. Excitement would come in its own time, as despair would have come if she had failed.

After finishing her second Martini, she left the bar and walked several blocks to the restaurant where she had gone previously with Tyler. She ate alone in the restaurant, and then she returned to her apartment, and it was almost eight o'clock when she arrived. She wondered what she could do until midnight, when Tyler would come, and she thought that perhaps she would sleep for two or three hours. She actually did set the alarm and lie down on the bed in the bedroom, but it was impossible to sleep after all. Lying there, she began to review in her mind all that had happened in the last hundred days or so since the death of Aaron, but this involved things about which she would rather not think. After half an hour she got up and went out into the living room and began to read a book called *The Sleepless Moon,* which she had bought only a few days earlier, about a man and a woman, married to each other, who shouldn't have been. At first it was difficult to get into the book, and her own thoughts kept interfering with the symbols on the pages, but after a while the symbols became dominant. She continued to read without stopping until the buzzer sounded at the door.

She looked at her watch and saw that it was ten o'clock, much too early for Tyler unless something had happened to change his plans, which wasn't likely. And even if his plans had been changed, it wasn't likely that he would simply come along early without calling first. Having considered and discarded the possibility of its being Tyler, she thought at once of Enos Simon, that it might be he at the door. If it was, which would be unfortunate to say the least, she had better see him and get rid of him quickly before Tyler came. While this was in her mind, she was aware also of a kind of subversive hope that he had indeed returned, was standing at that moment outside the door, and that she could somehow devise a way of salvaging him and making him compatible with the plan of her life, but this was impossible, as she knew very well, and was not to be seriously thought of.

But it was not Enos. It was a slender man, almost slight, neatly dressed in a dark brown suit with brown shoes and a brown knit tie, and he held in his right hand a brown hat that had covered, before he removed it, a head of short-cut light brown hair. At first she could not place him, though he seemed familiar, and then she remembered who he was, but she still couldn't remember his name, and this was possibly because it was a name she preferred *not* to remember.

"Good evening, Miss Buchanan," he said. "Do you remember me?"

"I remember who you are," she said, "but I don't remember your name."

"It's Daniels. The last time we met, which was also the first, I said that I would enjoy seeing you again, but we agreed that it would be impossible."

"Apparently we were wrong."

"Yes. Apparently. I hope you are not distressed about it."

"Why should I be? Are you here on police business?"

"In a way I am. In a way I'm not. The fact is, I'm delivering mail."

"What do you mean?"

"I mean that I have a letter for you. A note. May I come in for a few minutes?"

"If it's necessary."

"I regret that it is."

She stepped back and aside, still holding to the knob of the door. It was something of consequence, of course, that brought him here at this hour, and the chances were that it was unpleasant or possibly disastrous, though she couldn't think what it might be. What surprised her even more than his presence was the quiet readiness with which she would surely accept whatever it was that brought him. She watched him come past her into the room, feeling in her readiness a certain pride.

"Won't you sit down?" she said.

"Thank you."

He drifted across to the chair in which she had been sitting. Seeing her book, which was turned face down on the chair's arm, he turned toward her with the thin smile that she remembered well, now that she saw it again.

"I see that you are reading *The Sleepless Moon,*" he said.

"Yes."

"I haven't read it yet myself, but I've read a review. In the *Atlantic,* I think."

"The *Atlantic?*"

The question had an inflection of skepticism, and she regretted it as soon as it was spoken, not so much because it was a rudeness to him as because it suggested in her a naive snobbishness that discredited automatically the claim of a policeman to read anything superior to comic books. Sensitive to the inflection, he permitted his smile to return briefly.

"Anyhow," he said, "I'm sure you have no desire to discuss books with me at this hour of the night, or any hour at all. As I said, I have brought you a note, and here it is."

He took an envelope from his coat pocket and handed it to her, and she took it and looked at it, and there was nothing on the outside except her name. She had not seen Enos Simon's handwriting for years, not since the letters from college, and she didn't recognize it. But she knew just the same that the letter was from Enos and that he had written to her before dying and was by this time surely dead. This was knowledge that involved her awareness of the possibility, plus the presence of Daniels, and it was incontrovertible. Removing the note from the envelope, she read it quickly, the few lines, the simple statement of regret and gratitude.

It is too bad, she thought, *that he felt this way in the end. If only he had abused me or cursed me or made some kind of indictment, it would now be better and easier for me. He was weak or sick and in a very real sense a coward, though it was something he could in no way help, and if he has now killed himself, which he obviously has, it is because of these things and because he was simply not fit to live, and there is no good reason at all why I should hold myself responsible or be disturbed beyond the demands of compassion and natural sorrow, but I wish to God in all reverence that he had blamed me and cursed me and wished me dead instead of himself, for this would be something I could hold in contempt and soon forget, but I can never forget what he has written, not so long as I live, and he has done me after all the most harm that he could do.*

"So he has killed himself," she said.

"Yes. He cut his wrist with a razor blade and bled to death."

"I'm sorry, but I'm not particularly surprised."

"Aren't you? Why not?"

"Because he was a depressive. He went into the deepest despair over the slightest things, and he had absolutely no capacity for solving his problems."

"Well, some of us are like that, I understand. Did you know him long?"

"I knew him for several months a good many years ago. When we were kids. We met again this year and became friends again, but I have not seen him for about three weeks."

"Why not?"

"Primarily for the reasons I have indicated. He was not a person you could be casual with indefinitely. He became quite difficult."

"I see. Did you anticipate his suicide specifically?"

"Not specifically, nor particularly as a consequence of our relationship, if that's what you mean. It was merely something he might have done, for this reason or that, at one time or another."

"In fact, it was something he was almost bound to do. Is that right?"

"I think so."

"All right. So he did. He has committed suicide, as palpably as Mr. Burns died earlier this year of a heart attack, and that seems to be the end of it. It is only coincidental, of course, that you have been concerned in both instances—and I also, in a lesser way."

"Yes. Of course."

He looked at her without saying anything, and she folded the sheet of paper and returned it to the envelope and held it out to him. He smiled his thin smile and executed a small gesture of rejection.

"I thought you might like to keep it," he said.

"Don't the police like to retain things of this sort?"

"Only when they are evidence of something or other that concerns us. In this case, there doesn't seem to be any indication of that."

"Will it be necessary to give it any publicity?"

"The letter? Not adversely, at any rate. Certainly it can't be published so long as it is in your possession."

"Thank you."

"Not at all. And now I have intruded long enough. Good night, Miss Buchanan."

"Good night," she said.

He walked past her to the door and turned without opening it, and it was the last time that she saw his thin smile.

"When I left you about three months ago," he said, "I wished that I could see you again. Now I wish that I may never see you again on earth. The complications seem altogether too deadly."

He opened the door then and went out, and she turned and crossed the room to a table on which there was a glass ash tray and a package of paper matches. She set fire to Enos Simon's note with one of the matches and watched it burn to black ash in the glass tray. It was, in a way, like burning Enos himself. Like burning his body. As Aaron had burned to begin it, so Enos to end it.

Why did Daniels say that? she thought. *Damn him to hell, why did he say it? Certainly it is altogether absurd to think that I am, without wanting or trying to be, a kind of carrier of misfortune and death.*

She looked at her watch and read the time.

In an hour and a half, she thought, *it will be time for Tyler.*

MURDER OF A MOUSE

"Justice is blind," it's said, and so is vanity. This is the story of a man who learned it for himself.

His name was Charles Bruce, and early in the morning he got out of bed and padded into the bathroom. Even barefooted in pajamas he gave, somehow, the effect of almost frightening arrogance and vanity. His overdeveloped ego was apparent in the set of his polished blond head that was hardly tousled after a sleepless night. It lay exposed in the clean lines of a face that might have made him a matinee idol if he had possessed even the rudiments of acting ability. His vanity was, as a matter of fact, almost a disease. It approached narcissism. It was the kind of vanity that, when it has no particular talents to exploit, acquires in frustration a special evil. It is frequently found in criminals.

Moving quietly and quickly, he shaved, brushed his teeth and hair, made all use of the bathroom that he would need to make. When he was finished, he removed a hypodermic syringe from the medicine cabinet and loaded the barrel with a potent anaesthetic he had acquired with considerable difficulty. Carrying the loaded syringe, he went back into the bedroom.

His wife Wanda slept in peace, her lips curved in the slightest smile over protuberant teeth. Her hair, fanned untidily on the white pillow around her head, was sparse and a kind of dun color, the color of a common mouse. It occurred to him, as he stood looking down at her with the syringe in his hand, that she possessed many characteristics that combined to achieve that mouse-like impression — the hair, the teeth, an overall scurrying timidity that seemed to view the world with bright, apprehensive eyes. A strange sort of woman to have a million dollars in her own name. Tragedies sometimes develop from incongruities like that — a woman like Wanda with that kind of money. This thought occurred to him, too, in those final moments before he acted, but the thought stimulated in him no pity, no abortive remorse.

She was sleeping on her back, her left arm curled up around her head on the pillow. Her hand was turned palm upward, which exposed the soft underside of her wrist, and this made the job easier, of course. He could see without difficulty, even standing erect, a linear bulge of pale blue vein. He sat down beside her on the edge of the bed, and she sighed and stirred but didn't waken. Taking hold of the hand on the pillow and leaning his weight suddenly down upon her body, he slipped the sharp needle of the syringe into the soft flesh of her wrist and forced the plunger down.

She awoke with a sharp little cry, her eyes flying open with almost instantaneous understanding and terror, the understanding that what should have been the beginning of only another day was in fact the beginning of the last day. The initial cry repeated itself over and over, issuing from her throat like a pathetic, stereotyped plea, and her small body threshed futilely against the pressure of his. The anaesthetic injected, he placed both hands upon her shoulders and pinned her firmly, applying no more force than necessary and being careful not to dig into her flesh with his fingers. For he wanted no bruises. No signs of struggle.

The anaesthetic worked swiftly, and it was hardly any time at all until she slipped into an imitation of death that was, for her, a prelude to the real thing. He stood erect again, breathing deeply, sucking in and expelling air in a slow, rhythmic cadence. The needle, he saw, had torn the flesh of her wrist a little, but not seriously. The tiny wound would, as he had planned, be easily included in a later and larger one.

Turning away, he returned to the bathroom and ran cold water into the tub. While the water was run- ning, he unwrapped a new razor blade and laid the shining and deadly bit of edged steel on the lavatory in readiness. Then, watching the water rise slowly in the tub, he considered details. How would she do it? Would she sit in the tub in the water? The idea of the bloody water staining the flesh of her body was repulsive to him, and he was certain that it would be repulsive to her. It was something she wouldn't do, to sit in the water like that. No. She would be more likely to kneel beside the tub and let her arm hang over the edge. Or, better yet, she would sit. She would sit at one end, sidewise to the tub with her back against the wall, letting the arm hang over into the water. That would be the natural way, the comfortable way, the way she would probably do it if she were doing it of her own volition. Satisfied, he shut off the water taps and went back to her bed.

She was light in his arms. So very light. She must have weighed no more than a hundred pounds. Cradled in his arms, she looked like a sleeping child, her head dropping forward against his shoulder with an appearance of affection. Of this appearance, however, he was unaware. He was unaware of everything except the dominant necessity to do the thing right. In the bathroom, he set her on the floor in the position he had decided upon and recovered the tiny blade from the lavatory. He wiped it clean on a bit of tissue and put it between the thumb and index finger of her right hand. Holding it that way, between the two digits, he made the necessary quick incision in her left wrist and permitted the blade to drop free into the water. That's what would happen, he thought. She would certainly let the blade drop into the water.

Around her submerged hand and wrist, the water reddened swiftly, the depth of the color fading at its spreading fringe to a sickly pink. He watched for a moment the spreading stain, and then he left the bathroom for the last time. He left her for the last time, too, of course, but he felt no particular sense of parting. Even in the intimacy of marriage, he had been aware of her only vaguely as a person. Primarily as a symbol, a source of supply, a kind of million dollar personification.

He moved unhurriedly around the bedroom, gathering his clothes. He dressed with his usual fastidious attention to details, and the result of all this careful attention was, strangely, an effect of casual perfection, as if he'd just thrown his clothes on anyway and they had somehow assumed just the right drape and lines. When he was dressed, he packed an expensive leather bag with additional items of clothing and set the bag on the floor by the door through which he would leave. Crossing the room from the door, he sat down at a desk between windows and wrote a few lines on a single crisp sheet of paper, the top sheet of Wanda's stationery, which she'd touched, so that her prints were undoubtedly on it. He already had the lines formulated in his mind, and so he wrote swiftly: Dear Wanda, I've tried to be honest with you about Carol, and I'm trying to be honest now. We've decided to marry as soon as I can get free. I'm going to a hotel and will send later for the rest of my things. Please don't try to contact me personally, but I'll be happy to talk with your lawyer about a divorce. I assure you that I'll cooperate fully, and I'm very sorry if this causes you any distress.

He signed the note with his first name only and then crumpled the paper in his hand and dropped it on the floor, as it might have been crumpled and dropped by someone in a powerful emotional reaction. By a mousy little woman, for example, whose handsome and adored husband was leaving her. A pathetic little woman, really, in spite of a million dollars, who could find, in the bitterness of desertion and in the distorted satisfaction of a terrible recrimination, the final strength it would take to slash her wrist.

His lips twitched with a touch of irony at the idea of recrimination, and he went over and picked up his bag and left, locking the door of the apartment behind him.

Walking down the hall to the elevator, he was a picture of ease and well-being, one of life's lucky boys, broad shoulders and narrow hips accentuated subtly by fine tailoring. The rhythmic scissoring of his legs was crisp and certain but managed to convey an impression of effortless motion that contributed to a total effect of thoroughbred arrogance. He was a man whose mind was untroubled by intimations of misfortune or suffering or disgrace. He was a man to whom such things just didn't happen.

The elevator boy, who secretly hated his guts, smiled pleasantly with a professional regard for the side of the bread the butter was on. "Good morning, Mr. Bruce. Leaving us for a while?"

Charles glanced down at the bag in his hand and nodded shortly. "Yes."

His incisive monosyllable discouraged further questions, and the operator, watching the straight back, almost military in bearing, cross the lobby downstairs and exit through the street doors, compensated for the feeling of inadequacy Charles always gave him by calling him mentally a conceited bastard.

Outside on the curb, Charles waited a few moments until he caught the eye of a cruising cabby. "Ambassador Hotel," he said, and relaxed in the back seat. The cabby shot a glance at his reflected face in the rear view mirror, and he also, like the elevator boy, used mentally the word bastard. The term was prompted by a kind of impersonal envy, however, and was qualified by the word lucky instead of conceited. Some guys have all the luck. Looks and dough. Nothing on their minds but spending the next buck on the next beautiful dame.

As a matter of fact, Charles wasn't thinking of money and women at all. Not that he didn't think of them quite often. It was just, at the moment, that he was absorbed by another matter that had gained temporary dominance. Sitting there in the back seat of the cab, watching through glass the streets that assumed in the early sun a sparkling, deceptive look of cleanliness, he wondered how long it took for a life to drain away through a neatly opened artery in the wrist. He had for a moment a very vivid vision of darkening water, but he was, apparently, not disturbed by the vision. Looking out at the sparkling streets he didn't see, he even smiled a little now and then.

He was admitted to the lobby of the Ambassador by a doorman six and a half feet tall (all the doormen at the Ambassador had industrious pituitarics; this gave them a special look; in their vivid uniforms, a kind of Queen's Guard look) and he was relieved of his bag by a bellhop who looked like a sophomore out of the best frat in a good college, which was another calculated specialty of the Ambassador. At the desk, he was subjected to a cool appraisal by a cool clerk who might have been, from his appearance, a controlling stockholder in the corporation that owned the string of fancy hotels of which the Ambassador was one. Charles did not mind the appraisal. He was hardly aware of it. He was so used to acceptance, even privilege, that the possibility of anything else had ceased to be a concern in his life. He signed for a room and ascended ten floors with the bellhop.

Alone in his room, he unpacked his bag and disposed of the contents neatly. Then he put the bag in the closet and sat down for a cigarette. Reviewing his activity dispassionately to that point, he could think of nothing that he had done or failed to do that was sufficient to crack his calm assurance.

He had proceeded throughout with bold strokes. Except for the one major point of murder, he had been perfectly open. He had mentioned Carol in the note, and his affair with her could be verified by several parties, although he had been careful that Wanda herself had known nothing of it. He had been so open that no one, not even the most obtuse investigator out of Homicide, if it came to that, would suspect him of murdering Wanda for motives that could so easily be pinned on him. But he didn't for a moment really think that it would ever come to Homicide. The alternate was too credible. An ugly, neurotic little woman like Wanda and a man like him. Suicide, indeed, would be the *only* really credible disposition of the case.

But wouldn't she have taken steps to exclude him legally from inheritance? Wouldn't she have seen to it, in the end, that he could never touch that beautiful million? This, of course, was ridiculous. He smiled dreamily into the thin blue smoke of his cigarette, thinking what any competent psychiatrist would do to a contention like that. A shattered woman committing suicide in the intensity of neurotic anguish simply doesn't take time to tie up loose ends. If she was capable of that she would never commit suicide at all. No. She would do it as it would be assumed that Wanda had done it, quickly and blindly and without rational thought.

Having been open to this point, the strategy would be, of course, to continue that way. No reason at all, for example, why he shouldn't see Carol. As a matter of fact, it would strengthen his position as a man who had not tried to dissemble and had nothing to hide.

Passing to Carol, his thoughts lost their cool quality of detachment. They acquired, as they always did when she was their subject, heat and a certain wildness, reverting now to the remembrance of past instances in his relationship with her, and now pressing forward hotly to the anticipation of more to come. Carol, beautiful and hard and calculating. Carol, his kind of woman, stone and fire, remembered and anticipated in a hundred positions and places. In the soft and scented and designed clusk of a dozen fancy lounges with a thin stem of brittle glass between her scarlet-tipped fingers and her lips glistening from the touch of a martini or a daiquiri or a Pink Lady or whatever it happened to be at that particular time. In sand and sun with her golden-brown body barely broken by flimsy scraps. In other places when it was broken by nothing whatever.

At this moment she would be in bed, still asleep, her heavy pale hair shining on the pillow, her exciting body shadowed slightly by a haze of sheer nylon. Her lips would be parted, just barely parted, with bright enamel just visible between them, and the shadows of lashes that were real would be cast below closed lids. The imagery of her lying there like that was so strong in his mind, so real and so prescient, that he forgot completely, for a while, the image of the other woman who was still a pertinent factor in his life, the one sitting by the tub with her arm dangling in red water. The one who also slept, but differently and more deeply.

He sat in the room for perhaps thirty minutes, and then he went out and caught a cab, and within another thirty minutes he was ringing the bell of the door behind which was the reality of his imagery. It took her a long time to open the door, verifying the validity of his thoughts of her asleep, and when she finally came, she had pulled over the haze of nylon a second haze that did a little, but not much, to diminish transparency. He went in, and she closed the door behind him, and they met and fused in a spontaneous generation of heat that was a kind of emotional combustion. Her lips were restless and hungry, her hands and body aggressive in conquest.

After a while, hunger somewhat abated, she said, "Did you do it, Charles?"

"Yes," he said. "It's done."

"She's dead?"

"Certainly. You can't bleed freely very long and not die."

"Was it hard?"

"No. It was simple. Very easy. It went just the way I planned it." He went over to a table and helped himself to a cigarette from a silver box. He made no motion to light the cigarette but stood revolving it slowly between the fingers of his two hands. "The hard part is coming up. It'll take guts, darling."

She followed him to the table and took the cigarette from him. She carried it to her lips between index and middle fingers and waited with the cigarette still between the fingers until he had picked up the lighter that matched the box and furnished flame. She exhaled smoke in a long plume, and her lips curled around the cigarette in a quiet little smile that suggested some kind of amusing esoteric knowledge.

"Don't worry about my guts," she said.

He took one of her hands and held it palm up, stroking the palm slowly and softly. "Are you sure? Are you quite positive you can take it? Her supposed suicide will create a hell of a stink. We'll be torn to shreds. You know the things that will be said. Lots of people will call us a pair of murderers. Morally, that is."

"Morally?" She lifted shoulders to indicate what she thought of *morally*. "What about legally?"

"Legally we're safe enough. They can't substantiate anything by suicide. I doubt if they'll even seriously consider anything but that."

"What about the money?"

"It's all right, I tell you. The only thing that's left is to carry the thing through. If you play it wrong, if you say the wrong things or break down the least little bit, we're sunk. If we give them nothing more than they have now, they can never definitely establish anything against us even if someone gets an idea or two."

She turned away from him and crossed to the windows. Against the light, the double haze of nylon was nearly dissolved. He stood behind her, watching her, the pulses in his temples and throat throbbing suddenly and painfully like a trio of malignancies. She looked out into the bright light and spoke to him over her shoulder.

"Look, darling. You talk about my guts. You talk about my breaking down. I thought you knew me better than that. I thought you knew me as well as I've ever been known by anyone on earth. I guess I was mistaken, though, and so I'd better set you right. To look at me now you might not realize it, but I was one of seven kids. My old man was a leery bum, and my old lady was a whining slattern. I've eaten so damn much bread and potatoes just to fill my belly that I never want to see a potato or a loaf of bread again. I've worn cast-off clothes that weren't fit to wear wfhen they were new, and I've had rags against my skin that were so damn rough they gave me gall. I got me a philosophy early in life, darling, and there isn't anything in it, not one damn thing except what happens in bed, that you aren't supposed to pay income tax on."

She turned suddenly and faced him. "Look at me. I'm soft, aren't I? I'm lots of fun in the right time and place, aren't I? Just a soft, generous girl? If you got that idea, you're crazy. I want you all right, darling, I want you like hell, but I want you with a million bucks, and I wouldn't have you for keeps any other way. Now forget about my guts, darling. And forget about my caring a damn what anyone thinks or says."

He went over to her then, and she was soft, as he had known perfectly well she was, and she wras also hard, hard as a diamond beneath the softness, and he had really known that perfectly well, too. Not that he cared. He preferred it that way. It only made him want her more, because he was, after all, just the kind of man who would want a woman like that.

They used up an hour, and when he was ready to leave, he said, "I mentioned your name in the note. That means someone will probably be here on his way to me. When he comes, whoever he is, tell him I'm at the Ambassador, and I'll be there waiting for him. Open trail leading nowhere, that's the strategy, darling."

"When do you think they'll find her?"

"It's our maid's day off, so possibly not until morning. But it doesn't matter. It's all set up for them, whenever it is."

She touched the tip of a finger to her lips and his. "Okay. Whoever it is and whenever it is, I'll send him on."

He left her with that and went back to the Ambassador, and it was about nine hours later when he heard her voice again. The next time was on the telephone, and he was just thinking about going down to the dining room for some dinner when the bell rang.

He lifted the instrument and said hello, and she said, "He was here, darling. He just left."

"Already? Who found her? How did it happen?"

"I didn't ask. I didn't think it would be a good idea to sound too curious about things like that."

"All right. I'll wait for him here."

He hung up and waited, and it was only a short time before the desk rang up to tell him that there was a man from the police to see him. He told the desk to send the man up, and he waited the last couple of minutes in the open doorway to the hall.

The cop was a thin, middle-aged man with shoulders stooped almost to the point of deformity, and this seemed to make his arms hang down farther than normal, which gave him, in that one respect, a rather simian appearance. He took off his hat politely and spoke with a tired voice.

"Mr. Bruce?"

"Yes. Are you the policeman?"

"That's right. Name's Benson."

"Come in, please. I've been wondering what on earth you could want with me."

Benson walked into the room and turned as Charles closed the door.

"I'm afraid it's bad news. Your wife, Mr. Bruce. She's dead."

"Dead!" Charles gave a passable impression of shock. "She was all right this morning when I left. That is, I assume she was. As a matter of fact, she was still sleeping, and I didn't disturb her."

"Maybe you disturbed her a hell of a lot more than you thought, Mr. Bruce. Anyhow, she's dead."

Charles ran fingers through his hair and worked his features into a simulation of concern. "See here, Mr. Benson ..."

"Sergeant."

"All right. Sergeant. The point is. I may be somewhat responsible if Wanda's done anything..."

"We found the note."

"I see. Well..."

Benson cut across his words with a gusty sigh and said with quiet bitterness, "Look, Mr. Bruce. I'm not the one to explain it to. I'm just a guy running an errand. There's a big-shot lieutenant down at Headquarters wants to talk with you. He's the one, so if you'll just come along."

"Very well. I suppose there are certain formalities in these matters."

"That's right, Mr. Bruce. Formalities."

It was a short ride to Headquarters. The traffic was heavy, but Benson threaded the police car through it expertly, and they were there quickly. They found the lieutenant in a small room sparsely furnished with essential items, and he was a younger man than Benson, although he ranked him, and this might have been a reason for Benson's tired and quiet bitterness. The lieutenant's name turned out to be Tomlinson. He had a hard square face and competent square hands, and his brain was fairly effective, too. Next to being a lieutenant, he was proudest of knowing about things like predicate nominatives and how to use them. He studied books at home.

He introduced himself. "Thanks for coming, Mr. Bruce. I'm Lieutenant Tomlinson of Homicide." Homicide, he said. So it had come to that so soon. After the initial shock, Charles wasn't especially concerned, however. He imagined, thinking about it, that probably all suicides were at least perfunctorily investigated by Homicide.

He sat down and said, "Sergeant Benson tells me my wife is dead, Lieutenant, but that's all 1 know. I wish you would be kind enough to explain."

"Certainly, Mr. Bruce. I'll explain some things to you, and you can explain some to me. That's why you're here. Your wife apparently committed suicide."

Charles sagged a little in his chair, doing it quite effectively. He was silent for a moment, staring at the floor, before he spoke again.

"I was afraid of that, with the police concerned and all."

"Was that the only reason you were afraid of it? Because the police were concerned?"

"No. Sergeant Benson has told me that you found my note, so you must be aware of my grounds for fear. I may say in defense, however, that I never really thought she'd do it."

"Do what?"

Charles let his eyebrows rise in a brief expression of cold surprise. "Why, kill herself because I left her, of course."

"You think she did that?"

"It certainly seems very obvious."

Lieutenant Tomlinson shook his head slowly. "I don't think so." He kept on shaking his head, and his face seemed suddenly much older. "As a matter of fact, I don't think she killed herself at all. I think she was killed. Possibly by you, Mr. Bruce."

The sudden violent constriction in his chest was a kind of pain that Charles had never known. It was as though a powerful centripetal force had closed in upon his heart, and he wanted to cry out with the pain, but nothing of what he felt showed in his face. Not the least indication of it. There was nothing in his face but icy and arrogant disdain.

"You're insane," he said.

"Perhaps." Tomlinson turned side-wise and said, "Mr. Creely."

That was the first instant that Charles was aware of a fourth person in the room. The man called Creely stood up from his chair against a wall and came forward. He was about the same height as Charles but much thinner, with narrow shoulders, and he must have been twenty years older. He was dressed in a conservative gray suit that was obviously expensive, and he used the cane in his right hand, leaning upon it heavily, as if it were utilitarian. His face was deeply lined, beginning to sag a little from its frame.

Tomlinson said, "Mr. Creely's the one who found your wife."

Charles stood to face Creely. "How could that be so? I believe I know all my wife's friends, and this man is a stranger. If she was dead in the apartment, who let him in?"

"No one let me in, Mr. Bruce." Creely's voice was dry and precise. "I let myself in. With this."

He extended a hand, palm up, and lying in the palm was a key. Charles lifted incredulous eyes from the key to Creely's face, and he experienced a feeling that might have been terror when he saw the steady, virulent hatred in the man's eyes. It's always a shock to see hatred in the eyes of a stranger.

"I don't understand," he said.

"Don't you?" Creely's laugh was an arid whisper. "Surely a man like you has no difficulty in understanding the significance of a key to a lady's apartment. I used it discreetly, Mr. Bruce. Only on those occasions — rather frequent, I must say—when you were using the one you have to another lady's apartment."

Tomlinson cut back in, speaking slowly in a kind of cadence timed by the shaking of his head, "Your wife was apparently having an affair, Mr. Bruce, just as you were. Mr. Creely has been able to establish pretty definitely that he and your wife planned marriage. It seems she intended to tell you within a few days." He stopped talking, but his head kept right on shaking, and after a moment his voice picked up the tempo again. "So you see, Mr. Bruce, it isn't likely your wife would have killed herself because you'd left her. It isn't likely she'd have cared at all."

That was the wholly incredible thing. The thing that had never seriously crossed his mind. That she wouldn't care. Most of all, that she had planned to leave him—*him!*—for a gray, sagging, crippled specimen like Creely. And in the final phase of his destruction, with the terrible realization that the police would pin it on him since they knew Wanda was not a suicide, it was the cruel cut to his vanity that hurt him most. It actually drove him a little mad.

It took both Tomlinson and Benson to pull him off Creely.

www.ingramcontent.com/pod-product-compliance
Lightning Source LLC
Chambersburg PA
CBHW020653180626
46816CB00003B/1257